SAMANTHA SANDERSON

ON THE
SCENE

Also by Robin Caroll

Samantha Sanderson at the Movies

Other books in the growing Faithgirlz!™ library

Bibles

The Faithgirlz! Bible
NIV *Faithgirlz! Backpack Bible*

Faithgirlz! Bible Studies

Secret Power of Love
Secret Power of Joy
Secret Power of Goodness
Secret Power of Grace

Fiction

The Good News Shoes

Riley Mae and the Rock Shocker Trek
Riley Mae and the Ready Eddy Rapids

From Sadie's Sketchbook

Shades of Truth (Book One)
Flickering Hope (Book Two)
Waves of Light (Book Three)
Brilliant Hues (Book Four)

Sophie's World Series

Meet Sophie (Book One)
Sophie Steps Up (Book Two)
Sophie and Friends (Book Three)
Sophie's Friendship Fiasco (Book Four)
Sophie Flakes Out (Book Five)
Sophie's Drama (Book Six)

The Lucy Series

Lucy Doesn't Wear Pink (Book One)
Lucy Out of Bounds (Book Two)

Lucy's Perfect Summer (Book Three)
Lucy Finds Her Way (Book Four)

The Girls of Harbor View

Girl Power (Book One)
Take Charge (Book Two)
Raising Faith (Book Three)
Secret Admirer (Book Four)

Boarding School Mysteries

Vanished (Book One)
Betrayed (Book Two)
Burned (Book Three)
Poisoned (Book Four)

Nonfiction

Faithgirlz Handbook
Faithgirlz Journal
Food, Faith, and Fun! Faithgirlz Cookbook
Real Girls of the Bible
My Beautiful Daughter
You! A Christian Girl's Guide to Growing Up
Girl Politics
Everybody Tells Me to Be Myself, but I Don't Know Who I Am

Devotions for Girls Series

No Boys Allowed
What's a Girl to Do?
Girlz Rock
Chick Chat
Shine on, Girl!

Check out www.faithgirlz.com

faiThGirLz!

SAMANTHA SANDERSON

ON THE
SCENE

BOOK TWO

ROBIN CAROLL

ZONDERKIDZ

Samantha Sanderson On the Scene
Copyright © 2014 by Robin Caroll Miller

This title is also available as a Zondervan ebook.
Visit www.zondervan.com/ebooks

Requests for information should be addressed to:

Zonderkidz, 3900 Sparks Dr., Grand Rapids, Michigan 49546

ISBN 978-0-310-74247-0

Editor: Kim Childress
Cover design: Cindy Davis
Illustration: Jake Parker
Interior design: Ben Fetterley and Greg Johnson / Textbook Perfect

Printed in the United States of America

14 15 16 17 18 19 20 21 22 23 24 /DCI/ 10 9 8 7 6 5 4 3 2 1

For Isabella…
Because you're funny and smart and beautiful
and you inspire me.
Every.
Single.
Day.
I love you.
~Mom

CHAPTER ONE

"Then I just felt the *pop*. Next thing I knew, I couldn't even stand up." Jefferson Cole's red hair hung over his forehead, almost reaching his blue eyes. His voice hadn't deepened yet like some of the other guys' at Joe T. Robinson Middle School.

Samantha "Sam" Sanderson glanced over the list of questions in the Notes app of her iPhone. "Do you have any idea how your ankle got hurt?" she asked him. Sam was reporting on last week's seventh-grade game against the Pulaski Acadamy Bruins.

He shook his head. "Like I said, I was running to the end zone, was tackled, then felt my ankle snap. It took two guys to take me down. One of them landed on my leg." He lifted a single shoulder. "Coach said someone came down on it wrong."

"Bet it hurt."

"Like you wouldn't believe." The freckles seemed to jump off his face.

"You had to be rushed to the hospital?"

"I wouldn't say I had to be rushed to the hospital, exactly," Jefferson answered.

Sam gritted her teeth. He needed to work with her here.

It was bad enough she'd been assigned this story in the first place. Aubrey Damas, school newspaper editor and thorn in Sam's side, had given Sam this assignment, knowing full well that whoever reported anything negative about sports would have half the school upset with them.

Robinson Senators stood behind their team one hundred percent. That Sam was a cheerleader made her writing an article on the dangers of football even worse. Aubrey knew that and had given Sam the assignment on purpose.

"But you went to the hospital straight from the game, right?" Sam pushed. Having to be rushed to the hospital sounded a lot more interesting than he went to the doctor and was treated for an ankle fracture. Not really blazing the journalism world with this stuff.

"Yeah. Doctor says I have to stay in this soft cast for the rest of the week." Jefferson leaned his head back against his couch. "He said I have some tendon damage, so coach will probably bench me for the whole season just to be safe."

Talk about a flare for the dramatic. Sam turned her head so he couldn't see her grin. She glanced around the Cole's living room, noticing again the boxes piled in the corner. They were nearly hidden by the recliner, but she'd noticed them when Mrs. Cole had let Sam in. Probably Mr. Cole's things.

By now, most everyone at school knew the Coles were separated and heading toward divorce. Sam had overheard — for once, she hadn't been purposefully eavesdropping — one of the ladies at church mention that Mr. Cole had rented an apartment nearby. It was sad for a family to break up. Sam had been praying for them, especially Jefferson's sister, Nikki, who was on the newspaper staff with Sam. Nikki was Aubrey's best friend, which meant Nikki wasn't exactly friendly toward Sam.

Jefferson cleared his throat. "Dad says he'll talk with Coach after my cast is off. He told me he'd work with me every weekend to practice plays. Maybe I'll stand a chance of making the eighth grade team next year," he said. "I hope so. Man, I heard they might let some eighth graders play with the ninth graders next year, too."

"That's promising." Sam couldn't imagine being so fired up about being hit, but whatever. A lot of people didn't understand her passion to become a journalist.

Jefferson nodded. "Dad says it'll take a lot of hard work, but we can do it."

"I'm sure you'll make it." Sam didn't miss the emphasis on *we* ... was Jefferson planning on living with his dad after the big D? Nikki hadn't said anything about living arrangements. Then again, she didn't really talk to Sam. Because of Aubrey, Nikki and Sam didn't talk much. Still, Sam couldn't help feeling sorry for all of the Cole family.

"I'm studying both the seventh grade and eighth grade playbooks all the time. I nearly have everything memorized already. Dad says — "

"Who brought this in?" Nikki's voice rose above the music coming from the den where she'd been supposedly doing homework since Sam had arrived at the Cole house. She stormed into the living room, waving a piece of paper. "Jefferson, did you put this on the front door?"

Her brother tapped the top of his cast. "Seriously?"

Nikki turned her glare to Sam. "*You*. Did you do this?"

Sam started to claim innocence, but curiosity got the better of her. "Let me see." She stood and held out her hand.

Nikki thrust the paper at Sam. "You did this. You wrote this and left it at the front door, didn't you?"

Smoothing the paper, Sam read the single sentence, written in black, bold letters:

NIKKI COLE IS A FATTY

"Why would you do something like this? Are you the one making the calls, too?" Nikki's face turned redder than Sam's shoulders, which had been sunburned just two weeks ago. "Why? Why would you do this? Aubrey's right — you are jealous of us."

Jealous? Of Aubrey and Nikki? Oh, puhleeze. But that wasn't the issue at the moment. "Nikki, I didn't do this. I promise. I wouldn't do such a thing." This was just mean and nasty. Sam would never stoop so low. "You've gotten calls? What kind?"

"You're going to deny it?"

Sam shook her head. "Nikki, I know we aren't friends, but you have to believe me. You know I'd never lower myself to something like this."

Nikki paused, studying Sam for a long moment, and then she snatched the paper away. "Never mind. Just forget about it." She spun and stomped from the room.

Sam started to follow her.

"Don't bother." Jefferson's words stopped Sam. "She'll lock herself in her room to cry. Then Mom will go talk to her for a long time before ending up calling Dad to come have dinner with us."

He knew his sister's routine.

"Has she gotten notes like that before?" Sam sunk back into her seat on the chair across from the couch. She couldn't imagine someone writing such a thing, let alone deliver it.

But Jefferson nodded.

"Just like that?"

He shrugged. "Sometimes it says she's ugly. And she's

gotten a couple of text messages saying she's fat and ugly, too."

Text messages meant a phone number. "Has she recognized the phone number?"

He shook his head. "Nope. Dad tried calling it back, but it just rang until he got the recording that the voice mailbox hadn't been set up yet."

"What do the police say?" Sam's dad was a detective with the Little Rock Police Department, so she put a lot of stock in law enforcement investigations.

Jefferson's eyes widened. "We haven't called the police. Calling a girl fat and ugly isn't a crime."

Now it was Sam's turn to shake her head. "This is beyond just calling someone names. Texting and writing her notes, that can be considered bullying. All states have some form of law against bullying, so it actually *is* a crime."

"I didn't know that."

"Yeah. It can become real serious." She nodded toward the doorway Nikki had left through. "You see how upset that made her. Some people get stuff like that constantly. A lot of teenagers. Until they can't take it anymore." Sam didn't want to talk about all the documentaries she'd seen about how many kids had hurt themselves or worse because of one form or another of bullying. "Your mom or dad should call the police and report it."

"I'll tell them."

Good. Maybe the police could find out who was

behind this and catch them before Nikki got even more upset. In the meantime, Sam made a mental vow to pay attention to everyone around Nikki at school. "How long ago did this start?"

"Yesterday, I think." Jefferson answered.

Hmmm.

"Do you have any more questions about my injury?" Jefferson's question pulled Sam from her thoughts.

"Uh, no." She'd better get professional. If she wanted to be seen as a serious journalist like her mom, she had to act like a pro no matter how dull the assignment. She forced a smile and stood, slipping her phone into her backpack. "I think I have everything I need. Aubrey said Marcus had already come by and taken your picture?"

"He left just a few minutes before you got here."

The school paper's photographer was always on time. Sam didn't think Marcus had missed a deadline. Ever.

Neither had she, but she had the career goal to become not just a journalist, but the best. She'd wanted to be a journalist ever since she could remember. Following in Mom's footsteps and all. Her travels ... her experiences ... Sam wanted all that for herself one day.

"Well, thanks for the interview." Sam slung her backpack over her shoulder. "I'd better get going. I'll see myself out."

"Thanks. Oh, and please don't say anything about

Nikki's notes or texts. She gets mad if she thinks I've gotten into her business." Jefferson gave a weak smile.

Sam nodded. "I understand, but do talk with your mom and dad about calling the police. They have an anti-bullying department that can help. At least they could trace the number the texts came from."

"I will," Jefferson said.

Sam nodded, then let herself out the front door. Nikki only lived a couple of blocks from Sam, so she'd put off the interview until this afternoon. Her article was due tomorrow, but she wasn't worried. She didn't have any homework, so could easily write the article tonight.

Taking these less-than-awesome assignments and turning out a quality article was a right step on her career path. Great reporter this year, editor in chief next year. Then hello high school paper. The only way Robinson High School's newspaper accepted a freshman on staff was if they'd been the editor of the middle school paper.

Her mind kept as brisk a pace as her walking. Who could be sending those notes and texts to Nikki? Aside from her being Aubrey's BFF, no one had a reason not to like Nikki. Of course, there was no telling if Aubrey, and Nikki by association, might have said the wrong thing to the wrong person.

Was Aubrey getting notes and texts too?

The air outside was still. Sam's scalp felt hot under

her long, thick hair. If she stayed out much longer, she'd be sweating.

She sprinted across the yard to her garage door and punched in the code on the keypad. The mechanical door opened with a creak and a squeak. Dad needed to work on that. She'd have to remember to tell him.

She raced into the house. Chewy, her German Hunt Terrier, met her at the door, jumping and wagging her whole body. Sam chuckled, then let the dog out into the backyard before starting on dinner. This morning before school, she'd pulled one of the casseroles from the freezer and shoved it into the refrigerator. That meant it wouldn't take nearly as long to cook, so it should be ready just about the time Dad would get home from work.

When Mom was home, Sam would help her make casseroles that were easy to freeze and store. That way, when Mom was off on a journalism assignment, Sam and her dad always had home-cooked meals.

Tonight was one of those nights, but Mom was coming home next week.

Sam had just finished dumping the salad mix into the bowls when the front door opened. Dad's keys clanked into the wooden bowl on the entry table. "Hi, Daddy," she called out.

"Hi, Pumpkin." As usual, he went immediately to his and Mom's room to lock up his gun and badge.

She added dressing and cheese to the salads, then set them on the placemats on the kitchen table.

"Something smells good." Dad kissed the top of her head after he came into the kitchen.

"It's stuffed bell pepper casserole," Sam answered as she handed him the hot pads.

"No wonder my stomach's growling." He pulled the casserole from the oven and set it on the cooling rack.

She turned off the oven and passed him the silver server and two plates. He cut generous pieces of the cheesy, meaty casserole, then carried the plates to the table. Sam joined him, carrying two glasses of milk.

Dad said grace. Her own stomach growling, Sam shoved a bite of the hot casserole into her mouth. The yummy tomato and cheese flavors made her taste buds stand up and dance. She couldn't help making a little sighing sound.

Shaking his head, Dad laughed. "You enjoy your food like your mother."

"I'll take that as a compliment," Sam answered and smiled before taking another bite.

"How was school today?"

"Good. I interviewed a football player who got hurt in last week's game. He hurt his ankle and probably won't be able to play the rest of the season."

"Ouch."

Sam nodded. "He's not really happy about it." She could kind of understand. If she couldn't cheer for a season, she'd be pretty upset. Or, if for some strange reason she couldn't be on the Senator Speak staff for even a week, *that* would be a fate worse than death.

"How was your day?" she asked.

"Uneventful, the way I like it." Dad smiled. It was a nice smile. Her dad was pretty handsome, if she did say so herself. Dad's hair had turned salt and pepper, but the pepper was still winning the race.

"You're writing a feature on this football player?" Dad asked.

She nodded. "Just one article. It's due tomorrow, but I don't have any homework." She took a sip of the cold milk. Mom only let them drink milk or water with dinner. Every now and again, Dad would let her have a soda, which was a treat, but to be honest, Sam liked milk.

"I thought you had cheer practice tonight since you have a game tomorrow." Dad wiped his mouth with the paper towel folded beside his plate.

Sam shook her head. "Mrs. Holt said we needed the break so we'd be charged and ready tomorrow for the pep rally."

"Makes sense."

She just couldn't stop thinking about Nikki's notes and texts. "Hey, Dad …"

"Yes?"

"What are the laws about bullying here?"

"Why? Are you being bullied?" Dad's face turned

into his bulldog look — eyebrows drawn down, lips puckered tight. His cheeks even seemed to sink in.

"No, not me. Just someone I know." She finished off her milk, but her mouth still felt like it was stuffed with cotton balls.

"Sam, if you know someone's being bullied, you have to report it."

"She told her parents. I'm sure they're handling it." Well, maybe. Maybe Jefferson told Mr. and Mrs. Cole they needed to contact the police, if not the school.

Dad didn't release his bulldog expression. "Bullying is very serious, Sam. That's why there are laws to protect kids from being bullied. Here in Arkansas, bullying is a Class B Misdemeanor. People convicted of bullying, and that includes cyber-bullying, face up to ninety days in jail and fines up to a thousand dollars."

"Oh, I know it's serious." But she'd have thought the punishment would be more than just a couple of months in jail and having to pay less than a thousand bucks.

"You should encourage your friend to make sure her parents not only tell Mrs. Trees and other school administrators but also the police."

The principal of the middle school, Mrs. Trees, had zero tolerance for any type of misbehaving. Sam had no doubt she wouldn't allow any type of bullying to go on in her school.

"Let me know if you'd like me to speak to her parents," Dad said.

Nikki would flip her lid, and Sam would really be socially outcast then.

"I'll let you know. Thanks, Dad."

Even though she had no plans of telling Dad who was being bullied, Sam had every intention of finding out who was behind it.

CHAPTER TWO

Stuffiness filled the room.

The heat wave of late September in Arkansas caused the school to run the air-conditioner on high, but it never really got cool in the old building's wings. Sam fanned herself and stared at the teacher sponsor for the school newspaper. She'd turned in her article on time, and even Aubrey had seemed satisfied.

"I'd like to see some series features on topics of interest to y'all." Ms. Pape glanced around the classroom the Senator Speak staff used as their newsroom. "Hard topics, not just the fluff pieces." She nodded at Samantha. "We had a great start this year with the paper's blog on serious topics. I'd like to see that continued."

"Right," Aubrey tapped her pen on the notebook opened in front of her. "Let's discuss some ideas."

"How about a series on the lunch food?" Paul Moore,

an eighth grader who was all eyes for Aubrey, asked. "It's beyond gross."

"Too boring." Aubrey shook her head. "And complaining about it wouldn't do any good."

"Besides, we aren't going to use the paper as a sounding board for complaints," Ms. Pape said.

"What about a series on the dos and don'ts of dating?" Kathy Gibbs, another eighth grader, asked.

"Well ..." Aubrey started.

"No. Mrs. Trees has been adamant about what is definitely not allowed in the paper, and dating is one topic that's off limits," Ms. Pape said.

Sam licked her lips. "How about a series on bullying?"

"Bullying?" Aubrey asked.

Sam nodded and glanced at Nikki, whose face turned red before she dropped her stare to the floor.

"That's a serious topic," Ms. Pape said.

"We could focus on different types of bullying and different punishments." Sam sat up straighter in her chair. This was a really good idea, now that she'd just blurted it out. "I spoke with my dad about the laws against bullying. It's a crime."

Nikki lifted her gaze and locked eyes with Sam.

Sam didn't want to make Nikki uncomfortable, but what happened to her was not only just plain wrong, it was also illegal. If she could figure out who was bullying Nikki, maybe she could make them stop. Even if Nikki wouldn't let her help, the articles might be enough to make the bully leave Nikki alone.

Although, either way, Sam wouldn't rest until the person was discovered.

"I like it." Ms. Pape turned to Aubrey. "What do you think?"

Aubrey quickly glanced at Nikki. She didn't stare so long that everyone would notice, but just long enough for Sam to realize Aubrey knew about the notes and texts to Nikki. Maybe Sam had been wrong, and Aubrey was getting them, too.

"I think it's a good idea," Aubrey finally said. "Who'd like the assignment?"

Just about every hand shot up.

"You know, Aubrey, it was Sam's idea. And she does have a father who can give her information on the criminal side of bullying." Ms. Pape crossed her arms.

It was entirely up to Aubrey to decide who whould write the series. Even though it was clear Ms. Pape thought Sam should get the assignment, she would let Aubrey make the decision, right or wrong. That's how news people learned, she had lectured many times: by making the hard choices and living with the consequences.

"Well, since her dad's a cop and can provide information, I'll give *Samantha* the assignment." Aubrey stared so hard that Sam could feel her heat. "How many articles do you anticipate including?"

Sam ignored Aubrey's intentional use of her full name and scrambled for an answer — she hadn't thought that far yet. "Uh ..." Type of bullying, punishments, what to do if bullied ... "At least five."

Aubrey nodded. "Fine. I'll expect you to submit your blog pieces in the mornings before school. As always, keep your articles interesting and factual. If you don't, I'll give the stories to someone else. Understood?"

Sam nodded, her mind already racing. She needed to talk with Nikki. She'd keep her name out of it, of course, but she really wanted to focus on how Nikki was being bullied and how it affected her.

If she could get Nikki to talk to her.

Aubrey turned the discussion to upcoming assignments, but Sam tuned the conversations out. How could she broach the subject with Nikki without ticking her off? Sam had seen just a glimpse of Nikki's reaction when she'd been at their house and felt pretty sure Nikki didn't want to discuss the bullying with Sam.

Was she embarrassed? Probably, but she shouldn't be. It wasn't Nikki's fault — she was the victim here. Sam just needed to make her understand that and see that the last thing Sam wanted was to draw unwanted attention to Nikki.

"Ms. Pape?" the student worker's voice over the intercom interrupted all conversation in the newspaper classroom.

"Yes?" Ms. Pape answered.

"Could you please send Sam Sanderson to Mrs. Holt's room?"

"She's on her way." Ms. Pape waved at Sam.

Sam grabbed her backpack and rushed to her locker where she switched her books for the duffle containing her cheerleading uniform. Once she and the rest of the squad had changed, Mrs. Holt led them to the gym to warm up for the pep rally.

As she stretched on the mats in the gym, Sam forced herself to focus on the pep rally. She wasn't worried about the cheers since she could practically do them in her sleep. But the stunts they were doing today were new. Because of their difficulty, Mrs. Holt ordered the mats to stay on the gym floor. She'd told the squad over and over that if they didn't practice and concentrate, someone could get hurt. The two flyers on the squad, Remy and Bella, were nervous visibly.

The whole squad was comfortable enough with their version of the varsity hitch pyramid, but Remy and Bella were still a little shaky on their stunts. They could do them fine on the ground, but once they were hoisted into the air ... well, Sam just whispered a prayer that they wouldn't let the flyers fall. With just nine girls on the cheer squad, they only had Grace as a spotter for the stunts.

Marcus Robertson, camera in hand, waved at Sam from across the gym. As the newspaper photographer, he'd snap shots to use as fillers for the paper's articles.

She waved back then stood and began practicing the cheer movements with the other cheerleaders.

Sam smiled to herself. They were working together great as a team, exactly the way they should be.

Like the newspaper staff was supposed to work together. Or, now that Sam thought about it, like a marriage should. She couldn't stop thinking about Nikki being bullied, and her parents getting divorced, and now Jefferson hurt. Sam put Nikki on her mental prayer list.

"Great job," Mrs. Holt said. "Okay, hustle up. Everyone's starting to enter."

Sam gathered her pom poms and moved to center floor with the other cheerleaders. They shook their poms to the rhythm of the band's drum beat. She smiled as Makayla, her bestie for all time, entered alongside Lana and sat in the second row, right behind where the cheerleaders would sit.

Aubrey and Nikki strode into the gym like they owned the place. If Aubrey's nose got any higher in the air, she'd drown if it rained. They walked up to the eighth grade section, midway up the bleachers. Thomas Murphy, Billy Costiff, and Kevin Haynes all sat behind them.

Lin called the first cheer, and Sam moved in sync with the rest of the girls as they cheered for a Senator win over the Little Rock Christian Warriors. After the cheer, the head coach of the eighth grade football team, Coach Harris, headed to the microphone. The cheerleaders took a seat in the front row. Sam sat right in front of Makayla.

"Looking awesome out there, girl," Makayla whispered in Sam's ear. "All those practices have paid off."

"Thanks."

"Even though cheerleading isn't a *real* sport like karate."

Sam laughed. Their ongoing argument would never end. Since Makayla was deep into karate, she claimed it took more discipline, training, and dedication than cheerleading. Sam, of course, disagreed. It was a private, good-natured debate between them.

"Yeah, you keep on believing that, but we both know the truth," Sam whispered back as she spied Mrs. Trees standing against the wall, holding papers. Probably the names of the homecoming court nominees.

The football coach finished his *we're gonna win and win big* speech, and the crowd yelled like crazy. That was the signal for the cheerleaders to rush back to the middle of the basketball court. Sam whispered a prayer, then waited for Lin to call the pyramid cheer.

"Five, six, seven, eight."

And they were in motion.

"One, two, three, four."

They lifted Remy up with no problem. Sam glanced across to the other side: Bella was in the air without incident as well. Grace caught Remy's and Bella's feet, and Celeste ran and dropped into the splits in the front of the pyramid.

"Go Senators!"

Sam smiled as she held Remy's foot tight. Perfect! Not even a little wobble. Flawless teamwork. They broke pyramid and clapped to the formation for their stunts. Sam let out a slow breath before joining Lin and Missy to lift Bella into a full extension.

They swayed just for a second before Kate moved from back spotter to help them steady.

Bella lifted her left leg entirely above her head, grabbing her instep with her right hand. Then she pulled her left arm in front of her leg, holding it parallel to the floor.

Sam held tight but looked at the other team who had Remy up in the same position.

The crowd yelled and clapped, many of them stomping the bleachers.

They'd done it! They'd practiced hard, and they'd done it.

Sam and the other cheerleaders counted the dismounts, grabbed their pom poms, then moved into center court. Right on cue, the band started the school's fight song, and the squad began their pom dance.

With the last note of the song, the squad split apart with jumps, kicks, and a couple of cartwheels before returning to their seats as the principal took the microphone.

"Wow, y'all were awesome," Makayla told Sam.

Still a little out of breath, Sam smiled and nodded. All the squad's hard work had been worth it. She couldn't wait to see the pictures Marcus took. Maybe she could snag a copy to show Mom and Dad.

"Attention please," Mrs. Trees said into the mic. Her voice echoed across the gym. Everyone hushed.

"I have the nominees for this year's Robinson Middle School homecoming court."

No one moved.

"As we've instructed, the nominee with the highest number of votes will be named Homecoming Queen. The other five girls on the list will serve as her court."

Sam shifted so she could see Nikki and Aubrey. Last year, Aubrey had been the only seventh grader to make court. If Aubrey made queen this year, Sam didn't know if she could take it.

"This year's homecoming nominees are ..." Mrs. Trees unfolded her paper and slipped on her reading glasses. "From the seventh grade: Bella Kelly and Lana Wilson."

Applause filled the gym. Sam reached out her arm to nudge Bella like the other cheerleaders, then she turned and waved at Lana sitting two rows up, wearing the most surprised expression.

Mrs. Trees continued. "And the nominees from

eighth grade are Remy Tucker, Lin Chang, Frannie Tully, and Nikki Cole."

Not Aubrey?

Sam stared into the bleachers. Nikki's face was red, but she looked excited. Aubrey's face was red, too, but unlike Nikki, her lips were in a tight line, and her eyes were squinted into little lines. Her eyebrows were almost one straight line.

Yep, Aubrey Damas was mad at not being nominated. It didn't even look like she could be happy for her best friend.

Sam caught her bottom lip between her teeth. This could get very interesting.

While everyone was still clapping and whistling, Aubrey shot to her feet and quickly made her way down the bleachers and out of the gym. Nikki's eyes were wide as they followed Aubrey out.

Sam let out the breath she hadn't even realized she'd been holding. Oh, yeah, this could get very interesting indeed.

CHAPTER THREE

That's awful," Makayla gasped. "Poor Nikki."

Sam nodded, even though her best friend couldn't see her over the phone connection. "I know."

"Does she have any idea who's behind the letters and texts?"

"I don't think so." Sam put her iPhone on speaker so she could brush her hair while she talked. "If she did, I don't think she would have accused me when I was there. I emailed a local anti-bullying group with a request for some basic information for my series of articles. Maybe something will make sense."

"Sam, who would be so mean?"

"Usually I would think Aubrey since she's the meanest girl at our school, but she's Nikki's best friend." Although, Sam remembered, Aubrey hadn't really acted too concerned about Nikki's parents getting divorced.

"But Nikki did get a homecoming court nomination, and Aubrey didn't this year," Sam said.

"Surely she wouldn't be so unkind."

"Hello? Have you met Aubrey Damas?"

"I meant she surely wouldn't be so mean to her best friend. Besides, Nikki got the notes before today's announcement."

Sam finished brushing her hair and reached for her cheer bow scrunchie. "I wonder if maybe Aubrey found out early and started the notes and texts." Aubrey's expression at the pep rally filled Sam's mind. "No, wait, I saw her face. She was surprised and angry."

"So we're back to the question of who would do such a thing?" Makayla asked.

Sam straightened the bow at the top of her ponytail, then smoothed her cheerleading skirt. "I can't think of anyone who has anything against Nikki Cole. Can you?"

"Not really. Unless you count Billy Costiff."

"Billy?" Sam wrinkled her nose as she sat and pulled on her cheerleading socks. "He's had a crush on her since fifth grade. He wouldn't do anything like this."

"Well, earlier this week, I was in the counselor's office working when Mrs. Creegle called Billy in." Makayla was a student aide during a class period.

Sam stopped tying her shoe and stared at the cell phone sitting on her desk. "About Nikki?"

"I'm not supposed to say anything about who I see in the office or anything I hear."

"Mac, this is serious."

Makayla remained silent.

Sam sighed. Sometimes, her best friend's adherence to all rules was trying. "This could help us figure out who is bullying Nikki. It might be against the rules for you to tell me something you heard in the counselor's office, but it's illegal to bully someone. We're trying to stop a crime here, Mac." Yeah, that sounded good. Really good.

"Well … I don't know exactly what all was said, but from what I could make out, Nikki had reported Billy's unwanted attention to the office. A while ago, Mrs. Trees told Billy to back off."

"What kind of unwanted attention are we talking about here?" Sam finished tying her shoes. "His following her around like a little lost puppy?"

"From what I understand, he'd become almost obsessed. Not just following her around campus, but slipping notes into her locker and stuff like that."

"Wow. I didn't know that." Sam rubbed Chewy's head, right behind her ears. The dog leaned into Sam's hand. "So why did Mrs. Creegle call Billy to see her?"

"I'm getting to that. Be a little patient," Makayla chuckled.

It was no secret that patience was not one of Sam's greatest virtues.

"Mrs. Creegle called him in because she'd gotten

reports that he wasn't taking Nikki's telling on him well at all."

Sam stuffed her pom poms into the large end of her megaphone. "What's that mean?"

"I don't know all the details, but from what Mrs. Creegle heard, Billy has become withdrawn and is not participating in any of his classes, and he's skipped the two classes he has with Nikki every day since Mrs. Trees talked to him."

"Wow." Skipping school was bad enough, but just skipping certain classes? That was practically a guarantee of getting busted.

"Yeah. He really looked disturbed when he left Mrs. Creegle's office," Makayla said.

"When was this?"

"Sam!" Dad's voice carried down the hall. "We need to go, or you're going to be late."

"Just a minute, Daddy." Sam turned off her speaker and pressed the cell against her ear. "When did Mrs. Trees talk to Billy?"

"He was in Mrs. Creegle's office this week, so I'd guess last week or something."

Sam accessed her notes from her interview with Jefferson Cole on the iPad. She sorted through the file she'd shared from her iPhone.

"Sam!" Dad called.

"Coming. Just a minute," Sam replied, covering

the mouthpiece on the cell so she wouldn't blow out Makayla's eardrum.

"Hey, I'll see you in the morning," Makayla said. "I'm so excited."

"Okay. See you then." Sam disconnected the call and scanned her notes. According to Jefferson, Nikki started getting the notes this week.

That meant, it *could* be Billy Costiff. Sam didn't understand how he could go from being adoringly obsessed with her to being a bully in a week's time, but who knew with guys?

"Sam!" She heard his footsteps coming toward her room.

She turned off the iPad, grabbed her megaphone with poms inside, and headed down the hall.

Dad shook his head as he moved her to the garage door. "If you're late and get demerits, no blaming me."

"I won't." She tossed her megaphone into the backseat, then slipped in the front passenger seat and fastened her seatbelt.

Dad pulled his truck out of the garage, then steered onto the road. The garage door closed behind them, which reminded Sam.

"The garage door is making those squeaking noises again. So is the front door."

"Increasing my to-do list, or are you trying to get everything assigned before Mom gets home?"

She grinned. "Well, if you don't do it before she gets home, you know she'll hound you until you do."

"Very true. She can be a real bully about my honey-do list." Dad braked at the red light and glanced at Sam. "Speaking of bullying, I did a little checking this morning."

"Oh?" Maybe the laws had changed or the punishment had gotten stricter.

"There've been no new reports of any bullying from students at your school."

That meant Mr. and Mrs. Cole hadn't called the police. Apparently Jefferson hadn't been able to convince his parents of the seriousness of it all. Or . . . "Maybe her parents talked to Mrs. Trees, and she was going to handle it."

Dad shook his head as he turned into the school's parking lot. "New guidelines are if a school administrator or teacher receives a report of bullying, they *must* contact the police. There's been no report this week from anyone at Robinson Middle School." He eased the truck into a space and turned the key.

Nikki must have thrown a fit for her parents not to report it to the school even. "I don't know, Dad. Maybe they think it'll stop." She opened the truck door and pulled her megaphone from the backseat before shutting it.

He locked the doors with a press of a button on his keychain. "That's not the way bullying works, Sam. Very,

very rarely does a bully just stop without some form of intervention." He led the way to the football field gate.

"I'm writing a series on bullying. Maybe I can get her to open up to me about that."

"Good. Please encourage her to ask her parents to call the police. You can even have them contact me if they'd feel more comfortable talking to a parent as well." Dad stopped at the line and pulled out his athletic season pass.

That probably wouldn't happen, but it was sweet of him. Sam stood on tiptoe to kiss his cheek. "Thanks, Dad. You're the best. I'll see you at halftime."

"Get outta here before Mrs. Holt benches you."

She ran through the gate and to the cheer area where the rest of the squad was already stretching.

"Nice of you to join us," Lin teased.

Sam grinned. "Hey, you guys, congrats on all the homecoming court nominations."

"Thanks," Frannie said.

"Did you notice all but two of the nominees were cheerleaders?" Celeste asked. "And those other two are on the paper?"

She hadn't, but it was true.

"So, what's your point with that?" Lin asked Celeste.

"Just that cheerleaders and newspaper staff *rock*."

Everyone laughed as Mrs. Holt joined them on the asphalt beside the sidelines. "Okay, girls. Pregame pyramid is the Swedish Falls. Everybody ready?"

This pyramid was one of their easier ones. They'd been practicing it most all of the summer.

"Please welcome the Little Rock Christian Warriors to the field," the announcer called over the speakers.

The people sitting on the visitor's side stood and clapped for the football players in the blue and green uniforms running onto the field.

Sam and the other cheerleaders waited until the Warriors moved to their end of the field before running into the middle, right on top of the Senator painted on the grass. Lin called the cheer, and they clapped into position.

"The Senators are here." Lin and Kate moved to the center and faced each other, arms extended and hands on each other's shoulders.

Sam and Celeste crouched, giving Remy a foothold. "We have no fear. So sit and watch. We'll show you how it's done."

Sam and Celeste lifted Remy up until Remy held onto Lin's shoulders and extended her arms, her stomach parallel to the ground. "We can't be beat. 'Cause we're number one!"

Remy's hands set on Lin's shoulders. Celeste kept a grip as Sam took a big step backward and held Remy's extended leg. "Yeah, that's right."

Sam held Remy's left leg while Remy lifted her right one. Frannie and Grace mirrored them with Bella, letting Bella hold on to Kate's shoulder. "The black, gold, and white. We told you once, we'll tell you again."

Remy and Bella were both extended in the Swedish Falls position and each lifted their free leg. "C'mon Senators."

Celeste, Missy, and Grace ran to the front of the pyramid and dropped into the splits. "Go, fight, win!"

The home team fans jumped to their feet, clapping. "Go, Senators!"

Once the squad broke the pyramid, they tumbled and jumped, yelling for the Senators.

"Here come your fighting Robinson Senators!" the announcer called over the speakers.

The crowd cheered and clapped even louder while the cheerleaders shook their black and gold pom poms and moved back to the asphalt alongside the sideline. The band fired up the fight song, and the cheerleaders fell into perfect step in their routine.

After the fight song, Sam dropped her pom poms in the row with the others. She glanced up and caught Dad's salute. She smiled in response, then started to move to her at-ready position, but she spied Nikki sitting two rows behind Dad.

Nikki had her head bent, sitting alongside her mother, with Jefferson on the other side of Mrs. Cole, his leg propped up on the seat in front of him. Jefferson, who had popcorn and a cup in his hands, was grinning from ear to ear, chatting with Mr. Cole, who was sitting next to him. They looked like a happy, all-American family, not one that was breaking up.

Looks sure could be deceiving.

Sam let her attention roam over the area. Billy Costiff was nowhere in sight. There didn't seem to be anyone who looked particularly interested in the Coles. Wait a minute. Sam shifted to the right. Was that Thomas Murphy sitting catty-corner to Nikki and staring at her? Squinting her eyes against the setting sun, Sam caught a glimpse of his face.

Yep, it was Thomas Murphy, and he continued to stare at Nikki like Chewy stared at her bag of treats on the pantry shelf.

"Senators have won the toss and elected to receive," the announcer called over the speakers. The Warrior football players lined up to kick the ball, while the Senators stood ready to catch.

Thomas Murphy was an eighth grader who easily could've played any sport but didn't. Sam didn't know why not, but he had pretty epic muscle tone and killer blue eyes. A lot of girls in school had a crush on him. He was cute enough, Sam supposed, but he didn't really *do* anything at school. He didn't play sports. He wasn't in any clubs. He didn't participate in extracurricular activities. He was a little odd. But he was cute, Sam would give him that.

By the way he stared at Nikki, it was pretty obvious he thought she was cute too.

The Warrior kicker kicked the football, and the Senator receiver caught the ball at the goal line and ran. He dodged the first tackle, then the next, and kept on running. He strong-armed and blocked another tackle before he was finally brought down on the twenty-yard line.

"Our year, ready?" Lin yelled.

Sam and the rest of the girls moved into position. "Okay!"

"Senators strive to be the best … there is no team like RMS," Sam yelled and made the cheer movements. "We're here to fight, here to cheer, come on Senators, this is our year!"

The fans stood and clapped while the cheerleaders went through jumps and some tumbles. The Senator offense took the field, Kevin Haynes in as quarterback. Sam couldn't believe Aubrey wasn't here to watch him play.

Where was she? As editor of the school paper, she was supposed to be at every game. Not being nominated for homecoming court must have really upset her. So, who was covering the game for the paper?

Sam glanced around and saw Marcus near the fence between the cheering asphalt area and the walkway in front of the stands. He lifted his camera and pointed it at her, then lowered it and smiled. She grinned back. The photographer was on the job, but who was the reporter?

Sam tried to catch a glimpse up into the press box where the announcer sat, but she couldn't see anyone. Maybe Aubrey was hiding in there.

Two more plays, and the Senators got the ball into the end zone. Touchdown! The band started the fight song, and the cheerleaders grabbed their poms and fell into their routine.

As she danced, Sam studied Nikki. With her head still bent to the tablet in her lap, she looked anything but happy to be at the game. Jefferson, on the other had, looked ecstatic. Then again, he wasn't the one being bullied.

Sam kicked, step-ball-changed, then kicked again. Maybe on her break at halftime she could talk to Nikki alone. If nothing else, she could let Nikki know that she was there for her if she needed to talk. Especially because, by all appearances, it looked like Aubrey wasn't going to be much of a friend.

CHAPTER FOUR

"Hey, Dad, do you mind if I go talk to a friend right quick?" Sam gulped down the water from the bottle Dad offered her during halftime.

"Sure, Pumpkin." That was one of the cool things about Dad. He didn't take it personally if Sam wanted to hang out with her friends. Or, as in this case, needed to talk to someone.

She gave him a quick peck on the cheek, then hurried over to where Nikki sat. She'd scooted further from her family, as if trying to pretend they weren't there. Or she wasn't here. Either one seemed to fit.

"Hi, Sam," Jefferson greeted her, all smiles.

"Hi," she answered but looked at Nikki.

Nikki frowned up at Sam. "What do you want?"

"Nikki!" her mother hissed. "Don't be rude."

Sam ignored the attitude. "I need to talk to you."

Nikki glared at her.

"Please." Sam softened her tone and her expression.

A second passed. Two.

"Fine." Nikki stood and turned to her mother. "I'll be right back."

Sam led her to the bottom of the stands, then over to the grassy strip beside the concession stand. The smell of hot dogs on the big grill wrapped around Sam and made her stomach growl. Mom always said the body would let you know what it needed. Right now, her body was telling her she needed junk food. Seriously. Too bad she had to talk to Nikki first.

"What?" Nikki turned, cocked out her right hip, and crossed her arms over her chest. "I don't have time for this. I didn't even want to come. Jefferson thinks it's great *family bonding*. Whatever."

Sam took in a slow breath to calm herself. It didn't work, because it only brought the smell of hot dogs in deeper and made her hungrier. "I want to ask you about the note you got while I was at your house."

Nikki blushed and shrugged. "Just some prank. That's all it was."

"And the text messages?"

Her face scrunched. "Jefferson has a big mouth."

"He wasn't telling me to cause a problem, Nikki. I think he's really worried about you."

"Shut up, *Samantha*. You don't know anything about me or my family."

If she thought using Sam's full name like Aubrey did would knock Sam off her game, she was in for a surprise. "No, I don't. But I know that notes like the one you got are a form of bullying, and that's illegal."

"I knew that's why you wanted to do a series on bullying. You want to use me to get attention, like you did with your last series in the paper. Well, I'm not going to play along. Just leave me alone." Nikki turned away.

"It won't stop, you know."

Nikki spun around. "What?"

Sam licked her lips. "My dad says that bullies don't just stop bullying. Once they get a target in their sights, they keep on doing it until they're made to stop." That wasn't exactly what he'd said, but it was close enough.

Dropping her arms, Nikki didn't look quite so defensive now.

Sam took a step forward. "Do you have any idea who could be behind this?"

Nikki hesitated, then shook her head. "It's only been for a few days, but it's ... I don't know how to describe how it makes me feel."

"Upset, mad, and a little scared?" That's how Sam would feel.

"Kinda." Nikki nodded. "I just don't know who hates me enough to do something like this." She blinked several times, the way someone did when they didn't want to cry. "I thought it was a prank, but this isn't just a one-time thing."

Sam knew the blinking trick all too well. She hated crying in front of people. It made her feel like she was weak or something. "How many notes and texts have you gotten?"

"I've gotten two notes — the one you saw and one before and about four or five texts."

Wow, that was a lot of contact for just a few days. "What do your parents say?" Even if Dad wasn't a cop, he'd have already called in somebody.

"Mom is more worried about if I really look fat, even if she doesn't come right out and say it. She told me I should wear clothes that weren't as loose fitting and wear things more straight-lined. Whatever that means."

What?! Sam gritted her teeth. Was Mrs. Cole blind? Nikki was smaller than Sam, and Sam knew *she* wasn't fat. "Nikki, you know that's not true, right? You're not even close to being fat, or even looking fat." What was wrong with Mrs. Cole?

"I know." But she didn't look convinced. Matter of fact, she looked really unsure of herself.

"You're not fat by a long shot. And you've got the support of the rest of the school, right? I mean, you *were* voted a homecoming queen nominee."

Nikki smiled, the first time since Sam started talking to her.

"I mean, that's pretty cool, right? Not everyone gets nominated. Even those who expect to be."

Nikki grinned. "You're talking about Aubrey."

Sam shrugged. "Hey, if the shoe fits..."

"She still hasn't talked to me," Nikki whispered. "Not since the announcement this afternoon at the pep rally." She looked over her shoulder.

Sam nodded. "I'm a little surprised she isn't here on behalf of the paper. I saw Marcus taking pictures."

"She passed it off to Paul." Nikki nodded at the dark-haired eighth grader sitting in the front row of the stands, notebook in hand.

"Oh."

Everyone knew Paul Moore had a huge crush on Aubrey and would do whatever she wanted, but he'd never covered the sports scene. Aubrey had always done the football game for her grade — Sam suspected it was so she could watch Kevin Haynes, star quarterback, in action.

Sam turned back to Nikki. "Look, I don't want to get all up in your business, but it's wrong for you to be bullied. I'd like to help."

Nikki narrowed her eyes. "But you're writing a series on bullying. At your suggestion."

"I know, and I'll admit I suggested it because of the note you showed me at your house, but bullying happens more than people know. I want to bring awareness to it." She took a step closer to Nikki. "And I want to help find out who is bullying you. Will you let me?"

"I don't want people to know. Especially now, with the nomination and all." Her blush returned.

"I understand." Sam glanced at the scoreboard's clock. She only had one minute to get back to the cheering area. "Look, I've gotta go right now, but I need to talk to you some more later."

"My cell's in the school directory. Call me."

Sam nodded, then ran off. Her feet were barely on the asphalt when the game resumed. Mrs. Holt glanced at her watch, then at Sam, her expression very clear: cutting it really close. The cheerleading coach was a nag about being on time. Tardiness was one of her major pet peeves and would land them demerits quicker than anything else.

Sam went through the motions of cheering, but she carefully watched Nikki take a seat next to her mother. Thomas Murphy was still sitting in the same place and still staring at Nikki as adoringly as Paul Moore stared at Aubrey. Sam almost laughed at the irony but caught someone else staring, then glaring. The new girl at school stared at Thomas, then followed his stare to Nikki. She shot the back of Nikki's head with such a hot look, it was a wonder Nikki didn't burst into a million pieces.

Finishing the cheer, Sam did a toe-touch, then a cart-wheel. She moved into her ready position but watched the new girl from the corner of her eye. She couldn't remember the girl's name. All Sam could recall was that she was in eighth grade and had just transferred to Robinson last month.

The Senators scored another touchdown. Sam grabbed her poms and fell into the dance with the squad as the band loudly played the fight song.

A transfer student would have to go through the counselor's office for scheduling. Sam smiled as she finished the routine and tossed her poms on the ground. She'd have to remember to ask Makayla about this girl who still threw knives at Nikki with her stare.

Sam thought about the note Nikki got. About the specific wording. *Fatty.* A girl would know that calling another girl that name would be really hurtful.

Yes, Sam would definitely ask Makayla about the new girl.

Saturday morning dawned bright, promising to be a hot day. Sam was more than ready for this day to get started. Nothing was better than spending the weekend with her best friend, unless it was spending the weekend with her best friend at Magic Springs/Crystal Falls in nearby Hot Springs.

"Ready, Sam?" Dad called out.

She gave Chewy a final rub, then handed the dog a

new rawhide bone to keep her busy until they returned that evening. Sam grabbed her beach bag and headed to the living room. "All ready."

Dad chuckled as he took the bag from her. "Did you remember the sunscreen?"

"Of course." She headed to the garage. "Did you remember to oil or whatever the garage door?"

"I did. This morning. While I had to wait on you." He unlocked the truck and tossed the beach bag into the backseat.

She quickly sent Makayla a text to let her know they were on their way.

The drive took less than fifteen minutes. After putting Makayla's stuff inside the bag, both girls crawled into the backseat of the king cab pickup truck, starting a gabfest for the forty-five minutes it would take to get to the amusement/water park in Hot Springs, Arkansas. Dad turned on the sports talk radio station he loved.

"Bet you were way excited that we won last night." Makayla took a sip from her water bottle. "I'm still bummed Mom wouldn't let me go to the game."

"Yeah, what's up with her lately?"

"Dunno. At least she's not still on her homeschooling idea."

Sam shifted so she was a little closer to Makayla, and she lowered her voice. "Speaking of school ..."

"What?" Makayla put on her *what are you going to ask me to do now* look.

"You know that new eighth grade girl that transferred in? I can't remember her name, but she transferred in after being expelled from another school."

Makayla nodded. "Felicia Adams."

Sam smiled. "Yeah. Her." She glanced at her dad in the rearview mirror. Good, his attention was on the curves of Congo-Ferndale Road and the radio. He wasn't wild about Sam being so nosy. As if he should be surprised. Hello, he was a detective and Mom an investigative reporter. "What's her story?"

"Why the sudden interest?" Makayla did the freaky eyebrow thing of hers, where she only raised one of them. That always wigged Sam out, and Mac knew it.

Sam shrugged, hoping she pulled off the casual look she aimed for. "Just curious."

"Samantha," Makayla growled, but kept her voice low enough that Dad wouldn't hear.

"I just saw her staring at Nikki last night at the game. It was more of a glare, really. I thought maybe she might be considered a suspect."

Makayla went silent.

"Mac?"

"Well, I'm really not supposed to say anything about what I see or hear in the counselor's office ..."

So there *was* more to Felicia's story. "Come on, Mac. I'm trying to help Nikki here."

"According to her records, she was expelled from Central Arkansas Christian for fighting. Mrs. Creegle said she's bitter about having to attend a public school and not being allowed to participate in any extracurricular activities."

"Really?"

Makayla nodded. "Apparently, she'd been a cheerleader and on the yearbook and newspaper staff at CAC, but when she got expelled, her parents told her she couldn't do any of that."

"And she got expelled for fighting?" In the public schools that would get you suspended but not expelled.

"It wasn't her first offense, from what I recall."

"Oh." That would do it. "So now school is a kind of punishment to her?"

"Yeah. I thought it was a little harsh, but Mrs. Creegle made notations that Felicia had some very serious discipline issues as well as attitude problems," said Makayla.

Sounded just like the type of person who'd bully someone.

Sam replayed what she'd seen last night in her mind. Felicia had glared at Nikki but had stared romantically at Thomas Murphy, who stared adoringly at Nikki. "You know, she might like Thomas Murphy, who I think has a crush on Nikki."

Makayla nodded. "Oh, he does. He tried to get his classes rearranged so he'd have more with Nikki. Of course, Mrs. Creegle didn't change his schedule."

"So, on top of just being mad at the world, Felicia

could also be jealous of Nikki because of Thomas, right?"

"I guess."

Jealousy could make a girl really mean. Mean enough to send ugly notes and texts.

"Hey girls, we're almost there. You have your passes ready?" Dad announced as he steered the truck off the interstate.

"Yep, we have them," Sam answered.

"It'll probably be packed since this is the last week-end it's open," Dad said.

"Until Magic Screams," Sam said. She *loved* the haunted houses the park put together. Epically scary.

Makayla shook her head. "I can't go there. The clowns!" She covered her face. "I'll never go again."

"Come on, Mac. They weren't *that* scary." But Sam had to admit, they were really, really creepy. Last year's clown maze of madness nearly had her screaming and running behind her best friend.

"They were too." Makayla shuddered. "I hate clowns. Always have."

"A lot of people are frightened of clowns," Dad said as he pulled in line to park. "I'm not sure why, but it's fairly common. It's called coulrophobia."

"Are you serious, Dad?"

"I am. So many people are scared of clowns that they named the phobia."

"Because clowns are just plain disturbing," Makayla said.

Sam laughed. "You're disturbing."

"Yeah, because you're disturbing me."

In just a few minutes, Dad had the truck parked, and they were on their way to the front entrance. The sun shone hot without a hint of a breeze. It still felt like summer.

After having their passes scanned and pushed through the turn stall, the girls rushed to the amusement park side, heading right for the big rides, namely the Gauntlet, Sam's favorite roller coaster. The big, yellow, metal ride had twists, turns, and loops — all while racing at over fifty miles per hour!

Sam tugged Mac's hand. "Come on."

Dad trailed at a much slower pace, carrying the refillable Magic Springs cups.

Mac rode the roller coasters with Sam, but that didn't mean she enjoyed it. It just proved what an awesome best friend she was. She stared at the line. "Do you see how long that line is? What, did everybody and their brother come out for the last weekend?"

Sam laughed and skipped to the end of the line. "I know it's long, but all the lines are gonna be that way. Just hang tough, okay?"

She grudgingly followed Sam, even though it was obvious she'd prefer *not*. "The line to the X-coaster is probably shorter. Why don't we go there first?"

"Come on, Mac. You just want to start off there because the ride is so much shorter." Sam tugged her into the line. "We'll go there next."

"We've ridden these rides so many times, I don't see why we can't just go straight to the water park. I want to go down the toilet bowl slide."

Sam shuddered. She didn't like the toilet bowl part of the slide. Something about swirling around a big, dark tub with water whooshing around wasn't the most fun for Sam, but she rode the big water slides because Mac loved them. "What did you bring for lunch?"

"A green salad, carrot and celery sticks, and grapes. You?"

Mac always ate so healthy. Not Sam. She liked *real* food. "Peanut butter and jelly sandwiches, Cheetos, and a banana."

The line moved up as another full load of screamers took off on the adventure of the Gauntlet.

"Hey, did you see this morning's paper?" Makayla asked.

"No, why?" What had she missed? Being a newswoman herself, Sam normally read the newspaper cover to cover every morning before school and church. This morning, she'd been so excited about the trip that she hadn't had time to look at the daily paper. She needed to make sure from now on that she allowed herself plenty of time. What kind of wannabe editor didn't even read the paper in the morning?

"There was an article in the business section about the layoffs at Hewlett Packard in Conway." Makayla shook her head. "About five hundred people have lost their jobs. Some of them have been there forever. Mom said in this economy, they might not find anything."

"Oh, man." Sam couldn't imagine what that would be like for a family. Her mom's reputation would pretty much allow her to keep her career going as long as she wanted. And Dad did a great job for the police department.

The roar of the roller coaster made the ground tremble as the car jerked to a stop.

Makayla took a step forward as the line moved. "Yeah. Mom's friend's husband was one of the ones laid off. She asked Mom to pray for them because they aren't going to be able to afford their house anymore and are having to move a family of five into an apartment."

"That's harsh." Five people in one apartment? Even if it was a two- or three-bedroom, it would still be very crowded.

Screams filled the air as the Gauntlet's riders were twisted and spun upside down.

"You know Melanie Olson, right?" Makayla asked. "It's her dad."

Sam vaguely recognized the name. "She's in eighth grade, isn't she?"

Makayla nodded. "Her mom told mine that she's not

handling it very well. Mom asked me to go out of my way to be nice to her. The whole family's having a really rough time."

Having to move from a house to an apartment — that would be rough. Taking two steps, Sam fell in behind the twosome in front of the line. The next Gauntlet turn, she and Mac would be on the ride and able to sit in her favorite place — right up front.

Wait a minute. The plant. "Hey, doesn't Mrs. Cole work at Hewlett Packard?" Man, if she lost her job on top of going through a divorce, Jefferson being hurt, and Nikki being bullied, that'd be terrible.

Makayla nodded as the Gauntlet came to a stop in front of them, the riders all talking and making it impossible for Sam to hear her until they exited. Sam jumped into the seat as soon as the attendant said they could. Mac followed.

"Nikki's mom is the one who had to do all the laying off," Makayla said. "I feel so sorry for her."

Sam's heart raced as the hard harness came down, but the anticipation and excitement for the ride wasn't the reason. "Does Melanie know Nikki's mom was the one who laid off her dad?"

"I guess. From what her mom told mine, Melanie is aware of everything. Why?" Makayla gripped the sides of the harness as the attendant gave the thumbs-up to the ride operator.

"Because if Melanie blames Nikki's mom, then she

could be the one sending nasty messages to Nikki in retaliation."

Makayla didn't have a chance to reply before the Gauntlet pinned them to their seats as it picked up speed. But just before Sam let herself go with the thrill ride, she made a mental note to try to find out how Melanie felt about Nikki Cole.

Sam's stomach freefell to her toes.

AHHHHHHHHHHHHHHHHH!

CHAPTER FIVE

This was awesome!

Sam couldn't believe she'd already heard back from the anti-bullying group she'd emailed Friday after school. They'd sent her several attachments of information. Scads of it. The director who emailed said she'd be happy to come talk to the school if the counselor would call her, and she'd even be happy to help set up a "no bullying" group of students.

That would just make Nikki madder than mad. She wanted to pretend it wasn't happening, but Sam knew things wouldn't get better on their own. Sam couldn't just ignore the reality.

"Sam, if you don't hurry it up, we're going to be late for Sunday school," Dad hollered.

She couldn't help that she'd gotten so distracted

reading the facts on bullying. "Coming." She shut her laptop and grabbed her iPad. She preferred her electronic version of the Bible. Chewy jumped off the foot of her bed and led the way into the hall.

Minutes later, she climbed into the front seat and clicked her seatbelt. Dad started the truck and immediately turned the air conditioner on high. "Mom said she'd FaceTime you tonight," he said. "If all goes well, she thinks she can grab a flight home tomorrow."

"Cool." She missed her mom but loved that her mom was a semi-famous journalist. It was one of the reasons Sam had gotten interested in becoming a journalist herself. Thinking about her mom got her to thinking about Melanie. "Hey, Dad?"

"Yeah?"

"Did you hear about all those layoffs at the Hewlett Packard factory in Conway?"

He nodded. "Pretty sad stuff. Lots of people lost their jobs." He cut his gaze to her for a moment. "Why? Did one of your friends' parents lose a job?"

"A girl I know at school. Her dad lost his job, and they can't afford their house anymore so they have to move into an apartment. She's pretty upset."

"I can understand that. Wouldn't you be put out if we had to sell our house?"

"Of course."

"There are a lot of people downsizing to more affordable homes." He looked at her as he stopped the truck at a red light. "We really need to be sensitive to their situation, as well as pray for everyone involved."

She nodded. "You don't think it was one person's decision to lay all those people off, do you?"

"Oh, of course not. Decisions like that are made by the company's board of directors. People who don't even live in Little Rock."

So it wasn't Mrs. Cole's decision to lay off everyone. Melanie shouldn't be mad at Nikki's mom, because it wasn't her fault. Even if she was the one who actually told everyone they were laid off. But maybe Melanie didn't understand all that.

Dad parked the truck and turned off the engine. Sam was out in a flash. "See you after Sunday school," she told Dad before running toward the youth room, iPad under her arm.

West Little Rock Christian Church stood off Cantrell/Highway 10, drawing attention with its beautiful and oversized stained glass front. Sam didn't know how old the church was, but she'd been attending since she was born. It was like a second home to her.

Sam ran down the hallway toward the youth room where Ms. Martha held Sunday school, anxious to tell Makayla what Dad had said about Nikki's mom and the layoffs. She also wanted to tell her about the anti-bullying group.

"Slow down, Samantha Sanderson," a familiar woman's voice rang out.

Sam skidded to a more sedate speed. "Sorry, Mrs. Kirkpatrick."

"What are you in such a hurry for?" The woman's pinched-looking face matched her nasally voice. Her beaked nose held her thick glasses in front of her eyes. She'd always given Sam a bit of the creeps.

"I just don't want to be late to Sunday school." Sam shifted her weight from one foot to the other, knowing it would be rude for her just to run off, but she really didn't want to stand there and have a conversation.

"Humph. Maybe you should leave a little earlier." Mrs. Kirkpatrick crossed her arms over her big chest.

No sense explaining. "Yes, ma'am." Sam flashed a big, fake grin. "Well, I'd better hurry along. You have a great day, Mrs. Kirkpatrick."

"You, too, dear."

Mrs. Kirkpatrick's smile didn't crack her face. Sam turned and rushed toward the youth room, careful not to run and get called out again. She slipped inside, passing Ms. Martha and a group of kids and headed straight for Makayla.

"Running late again?" Makayla asked, grinning.

"Don't go there. Mrs. Kirkpatrick just got on to me." Sam collapsed into the chair beside her best friend.

Makayla chuckled. "Running in the hall again?"

Sam nodded. "Hey, did you know there are like a gazillion forms of bullying?"

"Really?"

"Well, there are really only three main types: physical, verbal, and emotional, but there are a bunch of forms under that. Like cyber bullying, disability bullying, racial bullying … and a lot more I can't remember."

Makayla's chocolate eyes widened. "I didn't know that."

"Yeah. And did you know that all the schools in our district are supposed to participate in the Bully Proofing program?"

Makayla shook her head. "I've never heard of it."

"Me either, but we should have." Before Sam could say anything more, Ms. Martha moved to the front of the room while the rest of the kids took seats.

"Good morning," Ms. Martha said. "Let's open with prayer."

Everyone bowed their heads, and Ms. Martha prayed for them, the church, and the community, then started the Lord's Prayer for everyone to join together.

"Amen." Ms. Martha smiled across the group. "Today, I want to talk a little bit about Psalm 34:12–14. Turn to that in your Bible. Who wants to read it aloud for us?"

Sam tapped the Bible app on her iPad and typed in the Scripture reference.

"I will," Daniel said. He was the oldest of the group, a senior in high school. Sam liked how he always treated everyone the same, with kindness and consideration. He cleared his throat. " 'Whoever of you loves life and desires to see many good days, keep your tongue from evil and your lips from telling lies. Turn from evil and do good; seek peace and pursue it.' "

Ms. Martha nodded. "Thank you, Daniel." She sat on the edge of the table facing their group of chairs. "Those are some pretty powerful words, don't you think?"

Most everyone nodded, but no one volunteered anything.

"What do you think these verses mean?" Ms. Martha asked.

"Well," Lissi began, "to me, they mean we shouldn't tell lies and do wrong. Instead, we should do what's right."

"Good. Anybody else?" Ms. Martha asked.

Jeremy nodded. "I think it means we shouldn't do bad things or stir up trouble." Jeremy was one of the newest members of the group, the sixth graders just having been promoted to youth back in July.

"Good. Anybody else?"

"I'm focusing on the first part first," Sandy said. "The way it's worded, I get that it's meaning if we want to have a long life, we have to do the rest of it. Right?"

Ms. Martha smiled wide. "Very good. That is right. It's almost like it's a directive of something you have to do to live long."

Makayla lifted her head from her iPad. "The *don't tell lies* part is spelled out pretty clearly. But isn't that included in the *keep your tongue from evil* part?"

"True, I think it is," Ms. Martha said. "But I think

there's more to it than just instructing us not to tell lies. What do y'all think? What are some ways our tongues are evil, outside of lying?"

"Gossiping," said Ava Kate.

Lissi inched to the edge of her chair. "Spreading rumors."

"Good. Anybody else?"

"Talking about others, and tearing them down with our words," Sandy said.

"Right," Daniel said. "Even if it's behind their backs. That might actually be worse."

"Bullying," Sam said.

"Very good answers, everyone." Ms. Martha glanced back down to her Bible. "What about verse fourteen? What do y'all think it means to 'Turn from evil and do good; seek peace and pursue it.'?"

"I think it means if we hear anyone doing that kind of stuff — gossiping, talking about others, bullying — we're supposed to not be part of it. To go away and be friends with people who don't do all that," Lissi said.

"True — " Ms. Martha started.

"But that's not just it," Sandy interrupted. "The verse not only says to turn away from the bad stuff and look for peace, but it also instructs us to do good, too."

Ms. Martha nodded. "What do you think it means to *do good* in this instance?"

"Maybe it means for us to tell the person gossiping

or talking about someone that they shouldn't be doing that," Daniel said.

"Doesn't the Bible also tell us to stand up for those who can't stand up for themselves?" Makayla asked.

"Let's look at Proverbs 31. I think what you're looking for is there, Makayla," Ms. Martha said.

Pages fluttered, and fingers tapped on tablets.

"Here it is. Proverbs 31:8." Makayla read. "Speak up for those who cannot speak for themselves, for the rights of all who are destitute."

"What does this mean to you?" Ms. Martha asked.

"Well," Makayla began, "if I think about the verse in Proverbs when we're talking about verse fourteen in that Psalm, then I think it means if we know of someone who is being bullied or gossiped about, we're supposed to stand up for them."

Ms. Martha smiled. "Very good, Makayla. I think you are right. What are responsible ways we can stand up for someone being bullied or talked about?"

"We can tell the person talking about them to stop," Jeremy said. "Let them know that it's not okay to do what they're doing."

"We can report bullying to our schools' counselors," Sam said. "Every school in our district is supposed to be participating in the Bully Proofing program. There's a zero tolerance policy for bullying, and it's illegal as well."

"This is all very good. I'm proud of each of you. Let's all try to put Psalm 34:12–14 into action this week, okay?"

Ms. Martha closed her Bible and glanced at her watch. "Let's close in prayer before we dismiss to church."

Sam's heart pounded as Ms. Martha prayed. The youth director had picked verses that applied so closely to anti-bullying that Sam couldn't help but take it as a sign that that she was supposed to do the series on bullying and stand up for Nikki.

She couldn't wait to get started.

● ● ●

… but no matter the subcategory of bullying, those listed above or even those I've not included, it's all wrong.

And illegal.

What do YOU think? Do you know what the Bully Proofing program is? Did you know our school participates in the program? Sound off, Senators. Leave a comment with your thoughts. ~ Sam Sanderson, reporting

"I can't believe I've never even heard about this Bully Proofing program. Are you sure our school participates, *Samantha*?" Aubrey asked.

Monday afternoon and finally, finally there was a serious break in the heat wave with dark clouds hovering in the west. Last period couldn't have come any faster for Sam. Honors Math had been especially brutal, with ten extra problems assigned as homework, not to mention the essay she needed to write for English.

She most certainly wasn't in the mood for Aubrey Damas's sarcasm.

"According to the school board's website, every school in our district participates," Sam said.

"I wonder why there's no information up about it," Celeste said from the seat beside Sam. "We have flyers up on the bulletin board about every other thing."

"Maybe the bullies took them down." Paul Moore stared at Aubrey, standing a few feet behind her like a puppy dog. It was sad, really, the way he crushed on her.

Aubrey rolled her eyes. She knew Paul liked her, but she treated him like dirt all the time. Unless she wanted something. Then she was all smiles and goo-goo eyes. Sam thought it was beyond sickening.

"Mrs. Trees asked you to meet with her and Mrs. Creegle tomorrow morning, Sam." Ms. Pape smiled as she crossed the room to join the group. "She liked your idea of getting more anti-bullying information out to the student body and wants to discuss options."

Aubrey rolled her eyes again, as if Sam couldn't see her.

"Shall we go over the layout for the paper edition, Aubrey?" Ms. Pape asked.

Sam gritted her teeth as she watched them move to the editor's desk.

"I was bullied once," Tam Lee said softly behind Sam.

She turned in her chair. "Really?" Sam couldn't imagine anyone bullying the nice and smart eighth grader.

He nodded. "Yep, right after I moved here."

"I thought you'd lived here all your life." Funny how she didn't know that.

"Nope. I was born in Louisiana. Dad transferred from the Children's Hospital in New Orleans to the one in Little Rock when I was in third grade." Tam leaned forward in his chair, closer to Sam and Celeste. "My first week of school here, kids laughed and pointed at me. Made me feel like a real outcast."

Sam ached for the sweet little third grader Tam must have been.

"A couple of the bigger boys in the class would come up to me at recess and tell me to go back to China." Tam shook his head. "They didn't even realize I'm half Korean, not Chinese."

"That's awful."

"Oh, that was the nicer of the things they said. They called me several names in relation to my Asian heritage, all of them really mean and hurtful."

"How cruel!" Sam felt a twinge. Tam's experience had been many years ago, yet truth be told, there were times when ignorant people made racial comments about Makayla's African American heritage. Maybe things hadn't changed so much in the past ten years.

"What did you do?" Celeste asked.

Tam blushed. "I went home and cried to my mom, of course." He chuckled. "Mom called the principal, the teacher, and the school board. I'm really glad I was too young to understand the ruckus she raised, or I would never have been able to go back to school."

Sam laughed with him. She knew the feeling. When her mom got on a roll, look out. Joy Sanderson was a force to be reckoned with. Even Dad walked a wide, wide circle around her when she was riled up.

"Needless to say, the boys' parents got involved, and they didn't bother me again."

"Did they retaliate?" Celeste asked.

Tam shook his head. "I think they forgot about it rather quickly because we became good friends in fifth grade. Either that, or they didn't realize it was me who ratted them out. Anyway, it's all good now. We're still friends."

That meant those boys were some of the guys at their school now. Sam glanced around the room. They could even be in this class.

He stood, grabbing his laptop. "I just wanted to tell you that to let you know that bullying does happen, and I think you're doing a good thing in getting involved in awareness. Let me know if I can help you with getting the information out."

"Thanks." Sam watched him join Kevin and Marcus and some other guys in the corner. She couldn't help but wonder if either of them had been the bullies.

CHAPTER SIX

B^{am!}
    The slamming of the locker drew Sam's attention as she came down the ramp after school. Most of the bus riders had already cleared the breezeway, and the student athletes were changing in their respective locker rooms. Some of the car riders lingered around their lockers or the bathroom, but for the most part, the school day had ended.

Sam spied Nikki glancing up and down the breezeway. She caught a good look at Nikki's face: pale. She rushed down the steps and to Nikki. "What's wrong?"

"Did you see anybody around here? By my locker?" Nikki's eyes were wide, and her voice had a hint of panic.

Sam slowly shook her head. "But I wasn't looking for anyone. Why? What's wrong?"

Nikki's gaze darted up and down the now-deserted breezeway. "Look." She opened her locker. She pointed at the case of diet bars sitting on the shelf. "Those aren't mine."

Wow. The bullying had just jumped up to a whole new level.

"And they weren't here when I came to my locker before last period." Nikki kept looking around, as if someone would come out of the shadows and confess they were responsible.

"Okay." Sam needed to think. "Who all knows your locker combination?"

"Me and Aubrey. That's it. No one else." Nikki chewed the side of her fingernail.

Sam wouldn't put it past Aubrey, but she'd pretty much ruled her out as a suspect. Unless . . . well, unless someone else had done the initial letters, but Aubrey was taking it to this next level because of her jealousy over not being nominated. "Where is Aubrey? Don't you two normally go everywhere together?"

Nikki's frown was immediate. "She's been *busy* since they made the announcement of the homecoming court nominees."

Some best friend, but was she jealous enough to be so mean?

Sam figured she was, but for the moment, she should give Aubrey the benefit of the doubt. Besides, when would she have had time to put the box in the locker?

Then Sam remembered Aubrey *had* gone to the office to pick up Ms. Pape's mail during last period. She had time to do it then.

Plenty of time.

"I know she's happy for me," Nikki continued. "I do. I think she's just hurt she didn't get enough nominations and doesn't want to put a damper on my excitement, so she's staying away for a bit."

Uh-huh. Sam wasn't buying that. Nikki was too generous with her assumptions. Or maybe she just told herself that to make herself feel better about Aubrey stepping away from their friendship.

"Anyway, I don't know who could've done this." Nikki blinked several times. "I'm not fat." But she didn't sound so confident.

"Of course you aren't." Sam didn't know what else to say to convince Nikki that she didn't have anything to worry about in the weight department.

"Right." But Nikki still didn't look convinced.

"Is it possible someone could've gotten your combination by watching you when you didn't know?"

Nikki shrugged. "I guess, but they'd have to be really close, and I don't remember anyone getting that close to me. It would've freaked me out."

True. It wasn't exactly easy to see the locks unless

you were the one holding it. "Could you have forgotten to lock it before you came into class?"

Nikki chewed on her fingernail again. "I don't think so. I'm pretty good about locking it."

It was a long shot anyway. The bully would have been really lucky to have the box of diet bars in hand to put in Nikki's locker on the off chance she forgot to lock it.

It didn't make sense.

"Are you sure no one else has your combination? Maybe you gave it to someone to get something out of your locker once? Or you asked someone to grab a book of yours when you were absent?"

"It's too early in the year. I haven't missed a day. And I'm pretty positive no one else has the combination."

Well, there had to be a way the bully had gotten the combination.

Like someone could have given it to them. "I know Aubrey's your best friend, Nikki, and you want to believe the best about her, but is it possible, just maybe, that she gave your combination to someone else?"

"Why would she do that?"

Surely Nikki wasn't this clueless. Sam let out a slow breath, thinking fast. "Maybe she borrowed something and put it back in your locker? She could've been busy and asked someone else to do it for her. You know how she's always doing stuff like that." That was the truth. Aubrey would rather waste the time and energy to explain to someone where to find something or how to do it than actually finding it or doing it herself. It wasn't that she was lazy it was more like she felt it was her right to order people around.

Nikki gnawed on her nail. If she didn't stop, she wouldn't have any of her fingernail left. "I guess she *could* have, but she never said anything."

"Maybe it slipped her mind. Or she just thought it wasn't important or something."

"Maybe."

There wasn't much else in the way of explanation.

"I could ask her. At least then I'd have a name."

Or she'd have Aubrey even more mad at her. Sam didn't want Nikki to be on the really bad side of Aubrey. "She might not remember," Sam said. And if Aubrey was involved in any way in the bullying, she certainly wouldn't admit anything. She might even get worse if she thought anyone was close to figuring out her involvement.

Tears pooled in the corner of Nikki's eyes. "I just don't understand who could hate me so much."

Sam reached out and squeezed Nikki's arm. She remembered some of the information she'd gotten from the anti-bullying group. "I don't think bullying is about the person being bullied at all. I think it's about power."

"Power?" Nikki leaned against the wall of lockers. "Making someone feel bad makes the bully powerful?"

"No, it just makes them think they are."

"I don't understand how being hurtful makes you think you're powerful."

Sam struggled to recall some of the details she'd read. "Think about this: what if someone felt powerless in a certain situation. Like, at home. Their parents were mean or abusive or something. The kid would feel powerless, right?"

Nikki nodded, but her expression clearly said she had no idea where Sam was headed.

"She feels powerless to her parents hurting her at home and doesn't like it. So she hurts someone else by bullying them so she'll feel like the one who is in charge." Sam wrinkled her nose. "Something like that."

"I get it. Kinda." Nikki sniffed.

"Nikki, you have to report this to the principal. Mrs. Trees doesn't tolerate this kind of stuff."

"I can't. Not with the election coming up." Nikki pointed to a poster at the end of the breezeway, the one that read: Vote Bella for Homecoming Queen and make Robinson's court beautiful again. "The campaigning has already started. Mrs. Trees would make it a huge issue and that could hurt my chances of being elected."

"Is being Queen that important?" Sam didn't think so, but to girls like Aubrey, popularity was critical. She hadn't thought Nikki put such value on it, though.

"It would mean a lot to my mom. She got so excited when I told her I was nominated. She talked about dresses and tiaras. It was the first time I've seen her really excited since my dad moved out."

"Oh." Well, that explained a lot.

"Dad's been hanging out at the house more since Jefferson hurt his ankle. And now, since the announcement, he tells me I'm his princess and stuff and that he's so proud of me. I'm sure he's just being over-complimentary because of the letters and texts, but still ..."

Sam smiled. Her parents were proud of her for making good choices, getting good grades, and doing the right thing, but she didn't think they'd be over the moon if she were nominated to homecoming court. Not that she had to worry about that being a consideration.

Nikki blushed and gave a little smile. "I'm sorry to have kept you here so long."

"It's not a problem at all. I don't mind. I told you I would help you figure out who was behind this, and I meant it."

"Thanks. I really do appreciate it. Are you late to something?"

Sam glanced at her watch — school had dismissed over fifteen minutes ago. "Well, my neighbor is probably wondering why I'm not in the parking lot yet."

"Oh my gosh, I'm so sorry."

"Don't worry about it. She'll understand. Listen, you can call me anytime. Really. I'm serious about helping you." Sam rattled off her cell number.

Nikki wrote it down. "Thanks, Sam."

"I'd better run." Sam smiled, then turned and ran down the stairs. Mrs. Willis would be worried, for sure.

Sam liked their neighbor Mrs. Willis, even if she was hard of hearing and didn't see as well as she used to. She saw Mrs. Willis's old car in the back row of the parking lot as usual when Sam's dad had to work and her mom was out of town.

"Hello, dear. How was your day?" Mrs. Willis asked as Sam slid into the front seat.

The cracked vinyl nearly scorched Sam through her khakis. "Sorry I'm late. I got caught up at the lockers. Thank you for picking me up."

Mrs. Willis started the car, revving the engine like she always did. Sam suspected she needed to do that to make sure the vehicle was running. "It's no problem. I finished reading today's paper while I waited."

Sam knew Mrs. Willis was lonely. She was a widow after all. The whole way home, Sam talked about her day, cheerleading, school ... any and everything, right up until they pulled into Mrs. Willis's driveway next door.

"Thank you again for the ride," Sam shut the passenger door and slung her backpack over her shoulder. "I'm sorry I talked your ear off."

"Oh, dear, I loved hearing about your day. Remember, if you need anything, I'm right next door."

Sam jogged across the yard to her garage door. She

punched in the code on the keypad by the door. The mechanical door loudly opened. She gave Mrs. Willis a wave goodbye before heading into the house.

Chewy met her as soon as she walked inside, jumping and wagging her tail.

Sam laughed, dropping her backpack onto the entry bench and then bending over to love on her dog. Chewy licked her face while standing on her hind legs. She was one of Sam's bestest friends.

Sam took off her student ID badge and shoved it inside her backpack before heading into the kitchen. After she let the dog into the backyard, she opened the freezer and pulled out a casserole randomly. Nothing sounded good, but she knew Dad wouldn't be up to ordering pizza or grabbing something from a fast food place.

In her bedroom, she checked her messages. She had another email from the anti-bullying group with links to various websites that talked about bullying.

Sam thought about Tam's story, which got her thinking about incidents Makayla had that were similar. She just hadn't realized they were bullying.

Sam checked her Facebook page and saw a post from Nikki. Within a few clicks, Sam was scrolling through the posts and comments on Nikki's Facebook page but saw nothing unusual. There were a lot of recent wall posts to congratulate Nikki on her nomination. Sam took note that there were no posts from

Aubrey since Friday. There were plenty before, silly ones about shopping and eating, but nothing since Aubrey found out Nikki had been nominated for homecoming court and she hadn't been.

Makayla would never act like that toward Sam, and Sam certainly wouldn't treat Makayla that way.

Ring-ring-ring!

Sam jumped then grabbed her cell. Yeah! Mom was calling to FaceTime. Sam pushed the green button and waited for the connection.

In less than five seconds, Mom's beautiful face filled the cell phone screen. "Hi, my sweet girl."

"Hey, Mom. Where are you?"

"Stuck at a hotel by the Atlanta airport. My flight was cancelled."

Sam wrinkled her nose. "They can't get you on another flight?" She really missed Mom. Something fierce.

Mom shook her head. "Not until morning. I know, it's a bummer. I miss you, too." Sometimes, she seemed to be able to read Sam's mind.

Her mother was one of the coolest adults ever. First there was her mom's job — an international journalist. Her mom's passion for her career and her stories of the adventures she'd experienced filled Sam with the burning desire to have the same type of escapades. Not only that, but her mom was really pretty. Dark hair, smooth skin that barely showed even the slightest creases in the corners of her eyes, and perfectly straight, white teeth.

Sam wanted to be just like her when she grew up.

"Well, at least you'll be home tomorrow."

Mom smiled. "I will. So, tell me how school's going. What are you reporting on?"

She quickly filled her mom in on Nikki's troubles and the research on bullying she'd been doing for the series.

"Bullying's very serious, Sam. I'm proud of you for getting involved. That's not always an easy thing to do."

"It's got Nikki pretty upset."

"I bet. Maybe you could encourage Nikki to ask her mother to call the school or at the very least, talk to the school counselor."

"I tried." Sam rubbed her hands against her jeans, liking the tingly feeling in her palms when she rubbed them fast. "Nikki says her mom is more worried about if she really looks fat."

Her mom's eyes about popped out. "Oh, my! That's just not so. Mothers don't think like that."

"I said the same thing to Nikki, but she said her mother told her she should wear clothes that weren't as loose fitting. It made Nikki feel like her mom might think she is a little overweight. Nikki's going through a lot. Her parents are separated and divorcing."

"That's hard on a family. Especially a woman."

Sam nodded. "And her mom just had to lay off a lot of people at the Hewlett Packard plant."

"It sounds like she has a lot she's dealing with. I don't know Nikki's mother, but I feel for her. She's got a lot of emotional issues taking her attention at the moment. I'm sure she adores her daughter almost as much as I adore you."

Sam grinned. "You might be biased, you know."

"I am, and that's okay." Mom's smile could warm the room from across the many miles between them.

A noise sounded over the connection, like a door opening. Mom turned away from the camera for a moment, then was back, a big smile on her face. "I have to go, Sam. I'll see you tomorrow. I'll even pick you up from school, okay?"

"Okay, Mom. Love you. Bye."

"Love you, too, my sweet girl. Bye."

The video chat ended with a resounding beep. Sam cleared her cell phone and set it on the desk. She couldn't wait to see her mom tomorrow.

She ran down the stairs and let Chewy back inside, just as Dad came in. His keys jangled into the wooden bowl on the entry table. "Hi, Daddy," she called out.

"Hi, Sam." As usual, he went immediately to his and Mom's room to lock up his gun and badge.

"You just missed Mom. We were FaceTiming."

"Sorry I missed her." Dad planted a kiss on Sam's head. "She said she missed her flight."

Huh? Sam tilted her head. "She told me her flight was cancelled."

"Oh. Yeah." Dad sighed as he pulled the casserole out of the oven. "Right. Either way, she won't be home until tomorrow."

Sam narrowed her eyes and studied him while he cut the Mexican casserole. Something wasn't right. It was like he didn't really care about Mom not being home tonight. "Mom said she'd pick me up from school tomorrow."

"That's good, honey, but don't be too disappointed if Mrs. Willis or I show up instead." Dad carried the plates to the kitchen table.

Sam lifted the glasses of milk and followed him. "Why? Mom said she'd pick me up."

Dad shrugged as he sat down. "Flights get cancelled. Things come up." He took a sip of milk, then swiped the napkin over his mouth. "I just don't want you to be disappointed if Mom can't fly in on time again." He cleared his throat and bowed his head, then said grace.

Sam couldn't even concentrate on the prayer. What was going on? Dad acted like he was preparing her for Mom not coming home tomorrow. Had Mom's flight really gotten cancelled, or had she missed her flight? She replayed her conversation with her mom while Dad finished the prayer.

Mom sure seemed sympathetic to Nikki's mom about the divorce and work. And what had been the interruption that Mom sure seemed happy about, then had to get off the phone so quickly? Had someone come into the room? Who?

"So, how was your day?" Dad asked, yanking Sam from her thoughts.

"Okay." She shoved a bite into her mouth and chewed slowly to avoid conversation at the moment. She needed time to think. Time to process everything.

Because something surely wasn't right with Mom and Dad.

Sam swallowed, a burn scorching all the way to her gut as the obvious answer slapped her in the face.

Were Mom and Dad separating?

CHAPTER SEVEN

And a final reason for bullying is due to lack of attention from friends, parents, or teachers. This lack of attention can make a person bully you, just to feel popular and be seen as 'tough' or 'cool' and in charge.

What do YOU think? I'll be meeting with our school's principal and counselor to discuss what we, as a school and community, can do about bullying and will report back tomorrow. Sound off, Senators. Leave a comment with your thoughts. ~ Sam Sanderson, reporting

"I think you're reading more into the situation than there is," Makayla said.

Thankfully, Makayla's bus had been a little early to school on Tuesday morning, so Sam was able to grab her bestie and pull her into a corner in the cafeteria to talk about Mom and Dad.

Sam shook her head. "You didn't hear Dad. It wasn't just what he said, or didn't, but the tone of his voice. It was almost like he was totally disconnected."

"Maybe he just had a bad day at work. Or he's stressing about a case or something." Makayla squeezed Sam's hand.

"He's had bad days before and been stressed and didn't sound like this." Truth be told, she'd never heard him sound like he had last night. All through dinner, he'd steered all the conversation away from anything that had to do with Mom. Once Sam started paying attention, it became blatantly clear Dad didn't want to talk about Mom.

"I don't know, Sam. You should ask him."

Uh, no. "When I had time to think about it, Mom seemed odd, too."

"You said she was okay."

"But she seemed really to sympathize a lot with Nikki's mom going through a divorce."

Makayla smiled. "That's just your mom being nice. She's always like that."

"Yeah, but what about that interruption? I'm pretty sure it was a door opening and closing, like someone coming into the room."

"But you didn't see anyone, did you?"

"No, but Mom turned away to see whoever it was, and when she came back to me, she was smiling so big. She looked happier than I've seen her in a long time."

How had she not noticed before how her mom hadn't been happy in a while? Some reporter she was if she couldn't pick up stuff like that when it was right in front of her face.

"I think you're jumping to conclusions. Your parents are one of the coolest couples I know. They seem happy with each other, you, and life in general." Makayla smiled really big and wagged her eyebrows. "Except when you go off and do something that makes them crazy."

"I don't do that."

Makayla laughed out loud. "Yes, you do, but I love you for it. And your mom and dad love you, and each other. You're just being overdramatic. Stop seeing problems where there aren't any."

Sam frowned. "Maybe you're right." But she wasn't convinced. Mac didn't see Mom's face, didn't hear Dad's tone. Something was going on. Maybe not a divorce, but there was something wrong that hadn't been there before.

"I'm right. You'll see." Makayla gave Sam a quick hug, then pulled out one of those energy bars she was always chewing on. Sam thought they were gross. Period.

But the bar reminded her of diet bars. "Oh, I forgot to tell you about Nikki yesterday."

"What?"

Quickly, Sam told her best friend about the case of diet bars in Nikki's locker.

"That's just cruel." Makayla frowned. "I hope she's going to talk to Mrs. Trees about it."

"She's scared to because of her campaign for homecoming queen."

"That's silly."

"Well, not really." Sam explained about Nikki's mom. "So I can understand how she feels."

"But she can't just keep getting bullied. Those diet bars ... that's flat out mean. That goes beyond notes and texts calling her a fatty."

The bell rang. Everyone grabbed backpacks and books and headed toward the halls.

"I'm meeting with Mrs. Trees and Mrs. Creegle about our anti-bullying program this morning. Maybe we can come up with something," Sam said as she left the cafeteria, turning toward the office.

"See you in Keyboarding," Makayla answered, heading toward the opposite breezeway.

A whoosh of cold air slammed into Sam's face as she opened the office door.

Mrs. Darrington, the school secretary, stood behind her desk. "Mrs. Trees and Mrs. Creegle will be here soon. Go ahead and have a seat."

"Thanks." Sam slumped onto the bench in the front office. She glanced over the bulletin board. Flyers about clubs were posted, as was information on yearbooks going on sale and a notice about the TAG — talented and gifted — program upcoming events. Even an announcement for the Pathfinders counseling program. But not a single thing about the Bully Proofing program.

The office door slammed, and Felicia Adams stomped inside.

Mrs. Darrington sighed. "Why are you here this time, Felicia?"

"Dunno. Homeroom teacher sent me. Said she'd send a referral in a few minutes."

"Fine. Have a seat."

Felicia gave Sam an up-and-down look over before dropping onto the bench. She sat on the opposite end and twisted to face Sam.

And she stared.

To the point where Sam had the urge to fidget, but she wouldn't. Instead, she lifted her chin and met Felicia's hard eyes.

A long moment passed. Then another.

And another.

Finally, Felicia relaxed her posture a bit. "You're a cheerleader, aren't you?"

Sam nodded.

"And you're on the school paper, too, right?"

"I am."

"You're a regular do-gooder, huh?"

"Felicia, that's enough," Mrs. Darrington said.

"Hey, I'm just trying to get to know her. Make

friends. Fit in. All that stuff y'all keep telling me I need to do."

"No, you're being condescending and rude." Mrs. Darrington made eye contact with Sam. "Just ignore her."

Sam felt the burn of Felicia's stare rather than saw it. She lifted a shoulder, hoping she looked indifferent. "She isn't bothering me."

The phone rang. Mrs. Darrington pointed at Felicia. "You, behave."

Felicia put her hand on her chest with a dramatic flair. "Will I get a gold star if I do?"

The school secretary shook her head and answered the ringing phone.

Felicia chuckled under her breath. "So, do-gooder, I'm not bothering you?"

Sam turned to her. She forced her facial muscles to remain relaxed, even though her heart raced. "Nope. Sorry, if you were trying."

"Oh, if I was trying to bother you, you'd know." The roughness popped from Felicia's voice.

Sam shrugged again, forcing herself to stay calm. Where was Mrs. Trees?

"You're a cool one, do-gooder, I'll give you that."

Sam remained a stony statue.

The office door opened, and a student entered.

"What can I do for you, Chris?" Mrs. Darrington asked.

He held out a piece of paper to the secretary while he smirked at Felicia. "A referral from Mrs. Berry."

Felicia rolled her eyes.

"Thank you." Mrs. Darrington took the paper and scanned the information as Chris left, but not before he shot Felicia an ugly look.

"You cussed at a teacher, Felicia? Are you just trying to get expelled from here, too?" Mrs. Darrington made clucking sounds with her tongue.

"Gotta keep up my reputation," Felicia replied.

Mrs. Darrington just shook her head and went back to her desk.

Sam let her gaze fall to the floor. Where was the principal? Maybe she should go on to class and come back later. Mrs. Trees might've forgotten. Or maybe she got caught up in something.

"Is that shocking to you, do-gooder?"

Sam jerked her attention to the troublemaker on the end of the bench. "What?"

"Is it shocking to you that I cussed out a teacher?"

"Shocking?" Sam shook her head. "Just makes me feel sorry for you."

The other girl's eyes widened quite a bit. "Sorry for me?"

"Yeah."

"Why?"

Sam swallowed and let out a slow breath. Where was the principal when you needed her? "Because I think it's a little harsh to get the punishment you did for getting expelled, and I think you're acting out to get attention." She whispered a prayer that Felicia didn't knock her out. *Please hurry, Mrs. Trees.*

"Acting out, huh?" Felicia's eyes narrowed into little dark slits. "What do you know about it?"

Sam shrugged, praying she didn't look as scared as she felt. "Nothing, but that's just my opinion."

The back door to the office sounded, followed by the click-clack of heels on the floor. Down the counselor's hallway.

"Sam. Go on back to my office, won't you, dear?" Mrs. Trees smiled.

She stood and grabbed her backpack.

"You aren't so bad, do-gooder."

Sam walked off just as Mrs. Trees asked, "Felicia Adams, what are you doing in my office again?"

"I hope you have a plan of action, *Samantha.*" Aubrey met her as soon as she entered last period.

"A plan of action?" Sam set her backpack on the table next to Celeste.

"She's just irked that so many adults in the community have commented on your article on the school blog," Lana said in a not-so-quiet whisper.

Aubrey ignored Lana and crossed her arms over her

chest as she looked down her pointy nose at Sam. "You reported you were meeting with Mrs. Trees and Mrs. Creegle about what we could do about bullying. People are making suggestions. I hope you know that you'll be the one to answer their comments."

Aubrey sure was changing her tune. Not so long ago, Aubrey would have reserved the right to make the decision of who would respond to comments and what they would say. Apparently, this wasn't cool enough, so she'd pass it off to Sam.

"That's fine. We do have a plan of action, so to speak."

"What?" Ms. Pape asked as she came up behind Sam.

"One of our corporate sponsors is paying for an anti-bullying speaker to come give a presentation at the school next week, with a follow-up presentation for parents, teachers, and other adults in the community that night. Kids whose parents attend will get a free ticket to next Friday night's football game." Sam was pretty excited about what she, Mrs. Trees, and Mrs. Creegle had come up with.

"That's pretty awesome," Ms. Pape said.

"Who's the speaker?" Kathy Gibbs asked. "Someone famous?"

"A famous anti-bullying speaker?" Aubrey sneered. "Get real."

"Actually, the speaker is a best-selling author of books on bullying," Sam replied.

"Like any of us have needed to read *those* types of books." Aubrey grabbed her clipboard.

"You know, Aubrey," Sam moved to face her. "It's attitudes just like yours that make bullying the humiliation that it is. Awareness and understanding are the first steps in ending bullying."

"You think you know it all, *Samantha*?" Aubrey started.

"Girls," Ms. Pape interrupted.

Sam decided she'd take the higher road and just ignore Aubrey Damas completely. "Mrs. Creegle and I are also starting an anti-bullying campaign around campus. Posters, flyers ... everything we can think of to promote a no-tolerance policy to bullying and to promote the presentation next week."

"Very cool. Count me in to help," Lana said.

Celeste nodded. "Me, too."

"Well, that will give all you seventh graders something to do." Aubrey's smirk was as infuriating as her *I'm better than you are* attitude.

"I want to help, too," Tam said. "I can talk to Mrs. Shine to see if we can incorporate this into an EAST project."

"I'm in Tam's EAST class, too," Lana said. "Mrs. Shine is always pushing us to do more school and community-minded projects."

Aubrey's beady little eyes bugged.

Sam had EAST this year, too, but fourth period.

EAST was a class that focused on student-driven service projects by using teamwork and cutting-edge technology. The EAST classroom had the coolest computers, laptops, software and accessories, including GPS/GIS mapping tools, architectural and CAD design software, 3D animation suites, virtual reality development, and more. The kids in EAST could identify problems in the community and then use these tools to develop solutions, usually working with other groups.

"Oh, I'll talk to Mrs. Twofold about it. She always wants students in LSL to do some community service projects," Deena said.

The Leadership and Service Learning teacher, Mrs. Twofold, was very vocal in the school about the importance of getting involved in community service projects.

"Thanks, everybody. Mrs. Creegle is working on the details. She's going to send me an email tonight. I'll forward y'all the information."

"Sounds like a good plan of action. Good work, Sam," Ms. Pape said. "Aubrey and I need to discuss some assignments, so everyone get to work. Sam, as Aubrey asked, please review the blog and reply to the comments." She turned and led Aubrey to the editor's desk.

Nikki took a step closer to Sam. "Me, too. I want to help." Her voice was low, but Sam knew how much it took for her to volunteer.

This anti-bullying reporting was going to be big. Bigger than just the school. Bigger than just Sam's articles.

That stirring of the gut happened, and Sam recognized that she was onto something that would help her on her career path.

She had a simple dream: become a great international journalist. Her parents could probably afford to send her to the college of her choice, but Sam was determined to *earn* her way, and her parents' respect, by receiving a full scholarship to the University of Missouri, which was ranked as the top journalism college by Princeton Review. For the past three years, two students from Robinson High School, the high school Sam would attend, received full scholarships from Mizzou. But getting on the high school paper was quite the task. They don't allow freshmen on staff ... *except* for the editor of the Robinson Middle School's paper. That one freshman, they allowed onboard.

And Sam was determined to be that one. Even if it killed her.

CHAPTER EIGHT

Please let Mom be here.

Sam took the steps down the school ramp two at a time, clutching her backpack. Cheerleading practice had been brutal, but at least Nikki hadn't had any surprises in her locker after school. Sam knew — she'd dropped by Nikki's locker on the pretense of needing to make sure she had Nikki's current email address to send her Mrs. Creegle's notes.

The sun beat down on the school's parking lot. Sam squinted against the brightness, scanning the back row of the parking lot for Mrs. Willis's car. No faded paint caught the light, and Sam let out the breath she hadn't realized she'd been holding. Her eyes adjusted to the brightness, and in that moment she saw Mom's car and her mom's arm out of the driver's window, waving.

Relief washed over Sam, and she jogged over. Mom got out, holding her arms wide open. Sam stepped into her mother's embrace, and inhaled, drawing in the distinct scent of Chanel's CoCo, the only perfume Mom ever wore. Familiar. Comforting. Love.

"Oh, my sweet girl, I've missed you." Mom kissed her forehead.

"I've missed you, too, Mom."

"How was cheer practice?"

"Long. Tiring."

"Come on, let's head home and change." Mom opened the driver's door.

"Change? For what?" Sam climbed into the passenger's seat.

"Dinner. We're going out tonight for dinner. You've had enough casseroles for a while, don't you think?" Mom grinned as she started the car.

"Oh yeah." Sam adjusted the vents to feel the cold air blast against her face. "And I'm starving. Lunch was pretty bad today."

Mom laughed as she pulled the car out of the parking lot onto Highway 10. "School lunches usually are."

"When did you get in?"

"About ten this morning."

"Have you talked to Dad? Is he meeting us for dinner?"

The smile slid off of Mom's face. "I did talk to him. He's wrapping up a case and needs to work late. That means it'll be just us girls." She smiled, but Sam could tell it was forced.

Dad not meeting them for dinner? He usually got off early the first day Mom got back home so they could all *reconnect* as a family (Dad's word, not Sam's), but today, he was working late?

Words wouldn't form. Sam couldn't think clearly. She didn't know what to think. The possibility of her parents getting a divorce set in. Very real. Very scary.

And Sam couldn't find the way to open the conversation with her mom.

"So, tell me about the bullying series," Mom said.

Sam told her about the meeting with Mrs. Trees and Mrs. Creegle and their plan of action. Mom made a couple of suggestions and told Sam again how proud she was of her.

"Have you read the school's blog?" Sam asked as her mom turned into their neighborhood.

"I'm sorry, Sam, I haven't had time yet."

Sam swallowed her disappointment. She knew Mom had a lot of stuff to do as soon as she got home — she *knew* that, but Sam couldn't stop thinking that she'd gotten home about six hours ago. In six hours, she hadn't found the time to read a couple of online articles?

Sam couldn't stop the feeling that her mom didn't take her articles seriously. That was silly, because her mom was her biggest fan.

Mom whipped her car into the driveway, pressed the button, and the garage door rolled open.

"Hey, did you know Dad fixed the garage door's squeak? And the front door's, too."

"Oh, I didn't know they were making a commotion." Mom inched into the garage and turned off the car's engine.

"Yeah. I mentioned it, and he made a point to fix it before you got home."

"That's nice," Mom said as she led the way into the house. "Let's get changed. I've made reservations for six thirty at Arthur's."

Arthur's was the fanciest restaurant Sam had ever been in, and the food was amazing. The absolute best steaks, even better than Dad's, although she'd never tell him. Eating at Arthur's was a treat because of how expensive it was — they usually only went for special occasions like birthdays, Mom and Dad's anniversary, getting straight A's on her report card, etc. Sam couldn't remember a single time they'd gone to eat there just because.

They were going to Arthur's without Dad? What did that mean?

Sam hopped in the shower. Ten minutes and a lot of her vanilla-scented soap later, she quickly dressed in jeans and a nice shirt. Her mind couldn't quite wrap around what might be happening, and her heart pounded erratically at the possibilities. She loved her mom and dad, loved them together, loved them as a family. If that was about to end …

"You about ready?" Mom poked her head inside Sam's room. "We need to get going so we aren't late for our reservation."

Sam slipped on her dressy sandals, as Dad called them. "I'm ready."

Mom smiled big. "I'm excited to have a girls' night out. I have something I want to talk to you about."

A boulder the size of Little Rock lodged in the back of Sam's throat. Something she wanted to talk about? Was it the dreaded "D" word?

Sam followed her mom back through the house, into the garage, and slipped inside the car.

"I think we're going to have to order a soufflé tonight, too." Mom grinned. "Let's be decadent tonight since it's just us girls."

Sam nodded, only because no words could get past the dam at the top of her throat. How on earth would she be able to eat a thing? She certainly couldn't swallow. Even drinking water would be a special feat. *God, please help me.*

The drive only took a few minutes — they didn't even hit a single red light. Great. Even less time before the devastating news. Just great. They didn't have to wait to be seated either — their table was ready and set for them. The waiter lit the candle after handing them menus and placing black cloth napkins in their laps.

Sam couldn't concentrate. The words on the menu were all jumbled. The good thing was she always ate the same thing, so knew what she'd order: the Arthur's Filet, well done, with peppercorn sauce. She and mom would split the La France Triple Cheese Au Gratin potatoes and the sautéed green beans. All were her favorites, but right now, she didn't want to eat a single bite of any of it.

When the waiter appeared with their bread, Mom ordered sweet tea for both of them. Sam took fast sips from her water glass, pushing the lump down as best she could. "So, what did you want to talk to me about?" Might as well get straight to the point. *God, please help me get through this without making a scene. I don't want to be that girl who bawled and had to run outside.*

"Let's wait until after we order, okay?" Mom smiled, but even in the dimmed light, Sam could see the little tremors at the corners of her mouth, a tell-tale sign that she was nervous.

Which made Sam all the more nervous herself.

The waiter returned with their drinks, took their meal and dessert order, then left as unobtrusively as he'd come.

Sam drank water like she'd been crossing a desert for hours.

"Well, I'm sure curiosity is eating you up about now, huh?" Mom licked her lips.

Sam nodded and took another drink.

"I wanted to talk to you alone about this, without your father here, because I know you'll understand how much this means to not only me but to our whole family."

Sam set down her glass and gripped her stomach. All the water swished around, cramping and tightening.

"I know you'll also understand that I didn't make this decision lightly."

She was going to be sick.

Sam jumped to her feet. "I have to go to the ladies' room." She rushed to the little hallway and pushed open the door to the ladies' room. She caught sight of herself in the huge mirror over the sink to the right. Her face had flushed a deep pink.

She shoved open the first stall door, stepped inside, then shut the door, and leaned her back against it. Cramped in the small stall, Sam closed her eyes and concentrated on her breathing. Slow and steady.

God, please help me. I don't think I can do this. Not without having a major meltdown right here and now or puking everywhere.

Sam opened her eyes, then stepped out of the stall. She washed her hands and splashed a little cold water on her face. She'd better hurry back to the table, or Mom would come looking for her, worried.

She definitely didn't want to have this conversation in the bathroom.

With a final deep breath, Sam returned to the table.

"Are you feeling okay?" Mom asked.

Sam nodded. She planned to just keep her mouth shut and let Mom deliver the bad news. She concentrated on clenching her back teeth. Maybe she could keep the tears back that way. She absolutely hated to cry in front of anyone.

"As I was saying, what I'm about to tell you, I didn't make the decision lightly. There were many discussions with your father and a lot of prayer."

Just say it already!

Mom took a drink of her tea, then let out a long, slow breath. "I've been offered a special assignment from *National Geographic* to go and cover the unrest in the Middle East, parts of Asia, and other places. This is a very unique opportunity for me. Not only will I be the sole journalist on this trip to be featured in the magazine, but I'll also be able to get some truly meaningful information for the book I've wanted to write for years." She let out a long breath.

This was what she had to tell Sam?

"It's an amazing opportunity, and my heart is set on going, but your father is concerned because of the amount of time I'll need to be gone." Mom stared at her over the flickering candle and single red rose in the small vase in the center of the table. "I would be gone almost six months."

Sam finally found her voice. "Six months?"

Mom nodded. "There's a chance it won't take that long. Six months is the longest it would be for."

Six months without Mom?

The waiter appeared at their elbows and served their steaks and side dishes. The smell teased every tastebud on Sam's tongue. Her stomach even growled in agreement. The waiter left.

"Would you like to bless?" Mom asked.

Sam shook her head. How would she handle Mom being gone for six months? The most she'd been gone so far was two weeks, and Sam thought she and Dad would go bonkers.

Mom bent her head and said a quick prayer aloud. She lifted her head and stared at Sam. "What do you think?"

"You and Dad aren't getting a divorce?" The question popped out before Sam could stop it.

"A divorce? Heavens, no." Mom's hands froze over the au gratin potatoes. "Is that what you thought I wanted to talk to you about? Whatever on earth would give you that idea?"

Sam's face burned as she shrugged. She stared at her steak. "I don't know. Just that Dad said for me not to be disappointed if you didn't make it in to pick me up today, and you had someone come into your room while we were FaceTiming yesterday, and … well, I don't know."

Mom chuckled. "My sweet girl, I love your father

with everything I have, and he loves me. We don't agree one hundred percent on my taking this job, but that doesn't mean we don't love each other and aren't committed to each other and our family. We're praying, together, about this big decision."

A thousand waves of relief washed over Sam.

"Dad told you not to be disappointed because I had to fly on standby this morning. The flight the airline had booked me on wouldn't have gotten me home in time to pick you up." Mom smiled, her face lighting up. "But I was convinced I could get on an earlier flight, and I did."

Sam took a bite of her steak. The flavors burst inside her mouth. She couldn't resist smiling as she chewed.

"And someone *did* come into my hotel room. The representative from *National Geographic*. She and I shared a hotel room so we could discuss their final offer." She slipped a forkful of green beans into her mouth.

Sam swallowed. "Dad doesn't want you to go?"

"You know what a worrier he can be when it comes to keeping us safe. I think he'd prefer I not go to areas of civil unrest, but that's where the stories are." Mom's eyes lit up brighter than the flame on the candle on the table. "You know I've wanted to do a book on world conflicts for some time now. This would give me the chance to get the rest of the great research I'd need. When I got back, I could concentrate on putting together a book."

"But it's six months." Sam hated the whiney tone that slipped into her voice, but she couldn't stop it.

"I know. And that's why I asked Dad to let me take you out to dinner alone. To let you hear it from me." She took a sip of tea. "You understand why it's important to me, right?"

Chasing stories ... it was a life Sam wanted for herself one day. Of course, she envisioned her dreams happening before she got married and had a family. Would she be willing to put a career on hold for her family? Could she ask her mom to do that? "I do, Mom." Yet she was hesitant.

"It's a once-in-a-lifetime opportunity. It won't come around again." Mom finished her steak.

Sam chewed in silence. It wasn't fair of her to ask her mother to put her dreams on hold for her and Dad. But was it fair of Mom to put herself in danger and risk being taken away from them permanently? There didn't seem to be an easy answer.

The waiter came and took away their empty plates and refilled her tea. Mom ordered a cup of coffee.

Once the waiter left, Sam replied. "I understand why this is important to you, Mom." She picked at the crisp, white linen tablecloth.

"But?"

"I don't know." How could she tell her mom about

the battle raging inside her head and heart when she could barely understand it herself?

"I know six months sounds like a long time, my sweet girl, but in a lifetime, that's a very short time."

It wasn't just the six months. "Mom, what if something happened to you over there? You could easily get seriously hurt. Or worse."

"Oh, Sam … I know it's scary to think about, but we can't live our lives led by fear. Jesus never wanted that for us." She smiled. "I know you'd miss me, and I'd certainly miss you and Dad. A lot. A decision hasn't been made yet. I just wanted you to hear about the offer from me so you can be praying too, like Dad and I are."

The waiter showed up with the coffee and a Grand Marnier chocolate soufflé. He cut open the steaming chocolate and poured the heavy whipping cream inside. Even though she was full from the amazing dinner, Sam's mouth watered.

There was something so right about a chocolate soufflé with real heavy cream.

As if she could read her mind and understood Sam needed some time, Mom changed the subject. "So, tell me the story behind the story on your bullying series. Who's being bullied that you know?"

CHAPTER NINE

I just don't know how I'm supposed to feel," Sam told Makayla as she lay back on her bed, her iPhone stuck to her ear. "I want her to go because I get how important it is, but I don't want her to go because I'll miss her, and I'm worried something will happen to her. I need my mom." Sam groaned and rolled onto her side. "Does that make me selfish?"

Chewy licked her face. Sam laughed and pushed her away, so Chewy curled up on her dog bed and stared at Sam with her soulful black eyes.

"I don't think it makes you selfish. I think it shows you're human," Makayla reassured her. "And that you love your mom and don't want to be away from her or want anything to happen to her."

"I guess." Sam rolled onto her belly. "I know Dad's

more worried about her than anything, and that's why he doesn't want her to go."

"Is she going?"

"She and Dad are praying about it together. She asked me to pray too." Putting aside her own fears about her mom and her selfishness for wanting her to stay, Sam thought it was wrong that Mom would dismiss Dad's objections and move forward anyway. It didn't sound like something a wife should do.

Weren't couples supposed to compromise or at least get to a point where they accepted something? Sure, Mom said they were praying about it, but it seemed she'd already made up her mind.

"Bet it's not a lot of fun at your house at the moment."

"Not at all." Despite Mom and Dad loving one another and Mom reassuring Sam they weren't going to get a divorce, Sam could sense the tension between her parents.

That night she'd used homework as an excuse to go to her room, very uncommon for the usual first day after Mom got back from a trip. They'd usually have dinner together and then play a board game or just sit around and talk as a family.

Not tonight.

Tonight had been stilted conversation in the living room with the television on. Mom and Dad rarely watched TV when they were home together, unless it was the occasional movie.

"Hey, what did Mrs. Creegle decide about the anti-bullying campaigns?"

"I forgot to check. Hang on." Sam grabbed her Mac-Book and opened her email. With everything else, she'd completely forgotten to check.

Four emails loaded. The first one was junk. The second was from Mrs. Creegle. Sam began reading then said to Makayla, "She says she thinks we ought to have each grade come up with a slogan and anti-bullying campaign. We can make posters, flyers ... all kinds of stuff. It will be a contest. Whichever grade comes up with the best slogan will get free tickets to the home-coming football game. Whichever grade does the best with their campaign will get a special page in the yearbook."

"That's pretty cool. We have a lot of creative people in the seventh grade."

Sam continued to read. "Mrs. Creegle says she'll get the information on the morning announcements and wants to make sure I put it in the paper's blog."

"Sounds like a great idea."

"Yeah." Sam yawned and closed Mrs. Creegle's email.

"Did you see some of the homecoming posters already up?"

"I did. I saw one for Bella." Sam checked her third email. It was from Tam, reminding her to let him know what Mrs. Creegle said. She quickly replied by copying and pasting.

"Frannie's is really pretty and professional looking. I think her mom works at one of those printing places, so her poster is really good. Too bad she's in eighth grade, or we could ask her to help with the seventh grade campaign."

"True that." Sam noticed the fourth email was from Nikki. She clicked and opened it, gasping out loud as she read.

"What?"

"I just got an email from Nikki. Her bully emailed her."

"What'd the email say?"

"Hang on, she forwarded it." Sam scrolled down the page. "Oh. My."

"What?"

"Listen to this: You are so fat. Ugly. You were only nominated to homecoming court as a joke. Everybody knows that but you. Now you are the joke." Sam's gut twisted.

"That's horrible. What did Nikki say?"

Sam read aloud, "Got this and thought you might like to see it. Anybody could have emailed it since my address is in the student directory. Don't call. Dad's on his way over to look at the email with Mom." Sam hit the button to print a copy.

"You said she forwarded you the email?"

"Yeah. I'm going to send an email to the address that sent it." Sam clicked on the hyperlink and typed 'who is this?' before she hit SEND.

Whoosh!

"It's sent."

"Poor Nikki," Makayla said. "This is beyond cruel."

"I know, right?" Sam reread Nikki's personal words, trying to read through the lines to see if she could gauge how the bully's words had affected her. She couldn't.

Meep!

Sam glanced at her email. "Rats! My reply to the bully just bounced."

"Read through the message and tell me the reason."

Sam scrolled until she found it. "This gmail user does not exist."

"The email address was bogus."

"Somebody's clever," Sam said.

"What's the email address?" Makayla asked.

"It's," Sam right clicked to read the email, "*truthtelr-at-gmail-dot-com*."

"Hang on, give me a second." The clacking of Makayla's keyboard sounded over the phone. Sam was good enough on a computer, but Makayla was a true computer genius. Although she'd never tried her hand at "hacking," there wasn't much Makayla couldn't uncover on a computer. It was just the way her mind worked.

While she waited, Sam folded the printout of the

email and stuck it into the interior pocket of her backpack, then stretched, letting her feet rub against Chewy's back. Mom needed to take the dog to the groomer's for her final summer cut. Sam dug her toes into Chewy's thick fur. If Mom took her job, she wouldn't be here to take Chewy to the groomers or the vet. Or Sam to the doctor and dentist. Or come to any of Sam's basketball games.

"Just what I thought," Makayla's voice jerked Sam out of her misery.

"What?"

"Somebody created that account, sent Nikki the email, then went right back in and deleted the account they'd made."

"Really? You could tell that?"

Makayla chuckled. "You could, too, if you'd just take a few minutes to think about what you need to look for and where."

"I think I'd rather just ask you."

"Well, in this case, the person did the deleting almost immediately — less than three minutes after creating the account. This person wanted to be sure they didn't leave a digital trail back to them."

"That's insane."

"I know."

"So, there's no way for you to trace who opened that *truthtelr* account?" Another dead-end.

"If I had some better resources, I could find out. But

don't give up yet. Forward me that email, please. I want to try and track the IP address."

Sam nodded, even though Makayla couldn't see her over the phone, and forwarded the forwarded email from Nikki. "Okay, it's sent."

"Okay. Give me a little time to play around and see what I can come up with."

"You really think you can find out who sent the email to Nikki?"

"Maybe not who, exactly, but I'm hoping I can figure out where they sent it from."

"Oh, Mac, that would be awesome. You're such a genius."

"Yeah, I know. I'm a ninja genius, remember?" She laughed. "I probably won't be able to call you later. Mom's on a tear again."

Sam grinned against the phone. "On you about studying again?"

"It's not like I don't already have a perfect 4.0 from last year and so far this first nine weeks. By the way she acts, you'd think I was in danger of failing."

Sam laughed. "At least she isn't talking about home schooling you again."

"Shh. Don't give her any ideas." Makayla chuckled. "Anyway, I'll see what I can do, and we'll talk in the morning. Maybe my bus will be early tomorrow."

"I can always ask Dad to pick you up, and you can

ride with us." That would work. They could talk without anybody listening in.

"I don't think that's a good idea, Sam."

"Why not?"

"Well, your mom dumped a lot on you tonight. You said the three of you didn't discuss your mom's leaving tonight. I imagine your dad will want to talk to you about it when he drives you to school tomorrow."

"I hope not. I don't know what to say."

"Sleep on it. See how you feel about everything in the morning. I'll be praying for all of you."

Sam shut her laptop and plopped back on the bed. She stared at the framed picture she kept on her desk — the one of her and Mom, Dad, and Chewy at Christmas last year. They were all smiling, even the German hunt terrier. The picture of the perfectly happy family. That could all be destroyed, as much as Sam's mom didn't want to consider it.

"Maybe I can get Mom to drive me to school in the morning," Makayla said.

"Yeah." Sam turned away from the photo.

"I've gotta run. Mom will be in here in a little bit to check on my progress in Science. See you tomorrow. Hang tough, bestie."

Sam smiled. "Thanks, Mac. See you tomorrow."

Chewy jumped up on the bed and gave a little whine. Sam rubbed the dog's head, just between the ears like she liked it and stood. "Come on, I'll go in the backyard with you."

The dog pounced off the bed and followed Sam to the kitchen door. It was the funniest thing, Chewy being afraid of the dark. She hated to go outside at night to do her business unless someone stood by the door or went out with her.

Sam didn't mind tonight. The air had gotten much cooler, a promise of the fall peeking around the corner. Maybe the fresh air would clear her mind.

Or at least, ease the ache in her heart.

"Pumpkin, I know it's a lot to absorb about your mom. How are you feeling? Do you want to talk about it?"

Makayla had been so right.

Sam stared out the window. They'd barely gotten to the end of the street before Dad asked how she felt about Mom's leaving.

Truth was, she still didn't know. She'd tossed and turned most of the night, praying a lot as she tried to come to peace about the situation. Yet she was just as confused and torn today as she'd been last night. "I don't know, Dad."

"I understand. I really do. I'm hurt and confused about it all myself."

Something about hearing Dad admit he was hurt tugged at Sam. "Dad, I can't help feel like Mom's being a bit selfish in this decision. I mean, I know this is her dream and all, and I understand that, but . . . I don't know. I don't want her to go because I'll miss her. We'll miss her. We need her here. And maybe that's selfish of me." She hadn't planned to say all that, but the words just spilled out of her.

"I know. I feel the same way. I love your mother — she's my best friend in addition to being my wife, and I want to support her in her career because she loves it so much, and I think I've been very supportive . . ."

"You have, Dad. I've never heard you complain about her assignments and being gone a lot. I've heard you tell her how great she's done and stuff like that." She'd never considered before how Dad had to be affected by Mom's being gone so much. All the parenting duties were solely up to him, as well as his work stuff. Now that she considered it all, Sam couldn't believe her dad wasn't grumpy all the time. She needed to remember, so she could take it easy on him the next time they clashed over something stupid.

"Thank you, but I've truly never minded because your mom's always been so passionate about her assignments, and she's so good at what she does."

"She is." Which made the situation all the more difficult.

"So whatever you're feeling is perfectly

understandable. And natural. I'm feeling a lot of the same way."

Knowing that she wasn't alone in her feelings, Sam felt better. She also felt bad for Dad, who couldn't even complain to his best friend about how he felt, like she could to Makayla. "I'm sorry, Dad."

"It's not your fault, Sam. It's not really hers, either. It's just ... it is what it is, I guess." He glanced at her before turning onto Highway 10, and the sun hit his hair just right. Big chunks of his dark hair now shone like silver.

It is what it is. Sam hated that phrase. What did it mean? That just because something *was*, it couldn't be changed? Everybody just had to accept something because it was? That didn't make any sense to her.

Most importantly, she was tired of talking about it right now. "Dad, I don't know how I'm going to feel about this when I have time to really think it through. I'm still trying to absorb it all, you know?"

"Of course. I just want you to know I'm here for you. If you need to talk, whenever you're ready."

"I know." And of course it would be Dad there for her, because Mom would be gone. "Thanks."

She hated feeling like this! Hated that Mom had put them all in this position. And she hated that she and Dad were made to deal with this situation.

It was all so unfair.

He pulled up to the school circle. Sam grabbed her backpack, then leaned over and gave Dad a tight hug and kiss on his cheek. She got out of the truck before he could say anything. At this point, what could either of them say?

What if she and Dad just threw hissy fits to the point where Mom wouldn't go? She'd resent them forever for forcing her to throw away her big opportunity, which wouldn't be fair to Mom. But it wasn't fair for them to have to just accept it.

Maybe they could accept it, but would they be able to live with it?

CHAPTER TEN

"Where have you been? I've been waiting for forever." Makayla grabbed Sam's arm and tugged her to a corner area of the cafeteria as soon as Sam entered.

"How are you here so early?" Sam asked, setting her backpack on the table.

"I told you I was going to ask Mom to drive me. I told her I needed to go over a special project before school, which isn't a lie because this is a special project. It just isn't a school project, which I kinda implied, so maybe that means I lied after all — "

"Mac!" Sometimes, Makayla needed a little nudging to stay on track.

"Oh. Sorry. I'm just so excited."

"Okay, tell me."

"All right, but you have to be patient and let me explain."

Sam sighed but nodded. She'd obviously missed out on the patience gene in her DNA. "Fine."

"I went into the message source in the header from *truthtelr*'s email. From that, I got the originating computer's name and IP address. I used a GeoIP tool to look up the IP and found the name of it, so I went to *whois* and looked it up to find out who the owner is." Makayla's face was lit up like starbursts on the 4th of July.

Sam didn't care about the *how* of finding out, only what was discovered. "So, you know who sent the email?"

Makayla shook her head. "I can't find out exactly who sent the email. Not from the information I have."

So why was she so excited?

"But," Makayla smiled big, "I do know *where* the computer the email came from is."

Sam's own excitement built. "If we know where, then it has to be somebody who lives in that house, right?"

"The computer isn't at a house."

Sam's heartbeat quickened. "A place of business?" Oh man, that meant it was probably an adult. Although, there were a lot of kids who had part-time jobs, but they were usually high school kids. Was it a high schooler?

"It's here," Makayla whispered, her eyes wide.

"Here?"

Makayla nodded. "Here, at the school."

Sam couldn't say a word. Her tongue felt like it had swollen to three times its size.

Makayla leaned even closer, where her mouth was so close to Sam's ear that she could feel Mac's breath when she whispered, "In the EAST lab."

Sam could hear the blood rushing in her ears. "Someone sent Nikki that email from the EAST lab?"

Makayla nodded.

"Are you sure?"

"Positive. Unless someone pinged it, but I don't think so. The trace was easy enough for me to track. I think we're talking about someone who isn't such a genius."

"I can't believe that. That's insane."

"I'm not making it up," Makayla frowned.

Sam snorted and nudged her bestie. "Goof, I didn't mean it that way. I'm just surprised. And shocked. Who could do that?"

"Not only who, but how did they do it." Makayla pulled out a folded up piece of paper. "I printed out the email. Look at the time stamp of the email: 6:44 p.m."

"I didn't think anybody would be at the school at that time on a Tuesday afternoon. There were no games going on."

"What about football practice?" Makayla asked as she tucked the paper back into her folder.

Sam shook her head. "Practice is over by five thirty."

"A club meeting, perhaps?"

Again, Sam shook her head. "I was just in the office yesterday, and the club meetings were all posted. None were after school in September."

"Maybe Mrs. Trees had something going on?"

"It wouldn't have been anything the students were here for." Sam looked over the cafeteria. Kids grouped together, laughing and talking. "That would mean an adult was responsible. I just don't want to think that. I can't."

Makayla shrugged. "Then somebody had to break into the EAST lab."

"It's somebody in EAST."

"Maybe not. Someone else could've broken in. The little windows at the top. Anybody with a regular ladder could get in. Mrs. Shire doesn't keep it locked." Makayla had EAST, too.

"True, but they wouldn't know about the window being unlocked unless they were in the classroom. And," Sam theorized, "it had to be somebody who has a password on the computers, right?"

Makayla nodded. "They couldn't have gotten onto the server to email outside the school if they didn't have one."

"So it's somebody in EAST. It's the only answer that makes sense," Sam summarized.

"How would a student have been able to break in, though? They lock the gates on the breezeways. There's no way to get in the campus area."

"I think there is."

"How?"

Sam lifted her backpack to her shoulder. "Come on, let's see."

"We can't leave the cafeteria. Officer Bill won't let us."

"Trust me, come on." Sam gripped the strap of her backpack and headed past the stage, turned left by the soda machine, and up the stairs toward the media center. Just before the door to the media center, she turned right and went through the glass doors leading out to the blacktop and band room.

"We aren't supposed to be out here," Makayla whispered, but she followed anyway.

Ignoring her best friend, Sam walked to the right around the music room and up the hill toward the new baseball diamond.

"Sam," Makayla hissed.

"Come on." Sam stood at the front of the baseball diamond. She shielded her eyes from the morning sun. "Look, there." She pointed through the trees behind the diamond. "What's that?"

Makayla stepped beside her and looked where she pointed. "Is that a pole?"

Sam nodded. "I think it's a white pole, which means there's something right on the other side of those trees."

"There's probably a fence, though."

"I don't see a fence."

"It's probably on the other side, Sam."

"Let's go see." Sam took three steps along the side of the diamond.

"Hey! You two," Officer Bill hollered out from beside the outdoor basketball goal posts. "You aren't supposed to be out here. Come on down right now."

"I told you," Makayla said as she stomped beside Sam. "Now we're going to get in trouble."

"No we aren't. Just let me talk to him." Sam led the way to the security officer.

"Sam Sanderson, I should have known." Officer Bill shook his head. "What were you doing up at the baseball diamond?"

"Do you know what that white pole behind the trees is from?" Sam asked him. If they could identify the pole, then maybe she could figure out where to look on the other side to see if there was a way to get onto school property from there.

He looked in the direction of the trees. "Can't say I ever saw it. What were you doing up there?"

Sam shrugged. "Research for my next article." She forged on ahead. "Do you know if there are fences back there behind the tree line?"

"I don't know. Why don't you ask Principal Trees?" Officer Bill motioned them toward the ramp. "The bell's about to ring. You two stay out of trouble."

"Thanks, Officer Bill." Sam smiled at him, then linked

her arm through Makayla's and headed toward their lockers.

Brring!

The breezeway flooded with kids.

"That was close," Makayla said.

Sam wrinkled her nose. "Nah, I knew Officer Bill wouldn't report us. He's cool like that. We aren't the troublemakers."

"It was close enough for me. Speaking of trouble-makers, I didn't get a chance to tell you who Mrs. Trees pulled out of the cafeteria before you got here." Makayla stopped in front of her locker that was right next to Sam's.

"Who?" Sam opened her lock.

"Felicia Adams."

"What did Mrs. Trees want?" Sam hung her backpack on the hook, then pulled out her English and Math binders.

"I was close enough to overhear Mrs. Trees say something about Felicia destroying some of the homecoming court campaign posters."

Sam shut her locker and leaned against it. "I wonder if any of them were Nikki's."

Makayla shrugged and shut her locker. "Dunno." She pulled Sam out of the way of the other kids. "We have to talk about the email coming from EAST lab. We have to tell somebody."

"I'll let Nikki know. Maybe that will push her to tell her parents."

"Should we tell Mrs. Trees?" Makayla caught her bottom lip between her teeth.

"Nikki will never let us do that." A good reporter never revealed her sources. Even if the source was the victim. "We can't tell anyone without her permission."

"But it's illegal. Not just bullying, which that email most certainly is, but using school property to send it. I'm sure that's even more illegal."

"We don't have any proof."

"I'm positive, Sam."

"You'd be okay with explaining your tracking it down or whatever?" Sam put a hand on her hip. Makayla hated drawing attention to her epic computer skills. Especially if it meant getting called into the principal's office. It would be even worse now that her mom seemed to be the alpha mom of overboard parental involvement. "I mean, Mrs. Trees would probably have to call your mom in for a conference. Not that you did anything wrong but to just go over details."

Makayla narrowed her eyes and jabbed Sam in the arm. "Sam Sanderson, are you trying to manipulate me?"

Heat flamed in Sam's cheeks. "Is it working?"

Laughing, Makayla shook her head. "You're incorrigible, but, yeah, it is kind of working."

"Listen, let me see if I can get confirmation from

another source about a computer in EAST lab being used to send Nikki that email. I'll take it to Nikki and try and, uh, *manipulate* her into letting me at least tell Mrs. Trees."

The bell sounded, causing kids to slam their lockers and run to class. Everyone not in class in three minutes would be considered tardy and would have to report to the office to get a pass. An unexcused one. That would give Sam demerits in cheer.

"Okay?" Sam hugged her binders to her chest.

"We'll talk in third period," Makayla replied, rushing to her class on a different ramp.

Sam ran to the seventh grade ramp, the one at the back of the school. As she turned to go into English, she glanced over at the pathway to the baseball diamond. She'd figure out what that pole on the other side of the trees was. And if there was a fence or any barrier between the school and whatever that was. She stepped into the classroom.

Brring!

"Nikki, we have to tell someone. Whoever sent you that email broke into the EAST lab last night to send it." Sam sat on the edge of one of the tables in the newsroom.

"It doesn't matter where anybody sent it from." Nikki

glanced over her shoulder to make sure no one was close enough to hear their conversation.

Or was she looking to see if Aubrey watched? Sam let her legs dangle. Now that she thought about it, she could do some digging and see who all had solid alibis for last night during the time the email was sent.

"I don't want you to tell anybody. My mom and dad think it will die down. Whoever it is will move on to tormenting someone else if I just don't react."

"Do you really think it's okay to let someone else go through what you're dealing with?" Sam shook her head. "I won't use your name, Nikki. I would never, not without permission."

Nikki glanced toward the editor's desk where Aubrey and Ms. Pape carried on a deep discussion. "I don't want anyone to know it's me. I mean it. No one can know."

"I understand." Sam stared at Aubrey, too. "I'm curious if Aubrey called you last night or anything."

Nikki shook her head. "She still hasn't talked to me. I mean, she says hey and stands beside me at our lockers and sits with me at lunch and stuff, but she doesn't really talk to me."

Some best friend! It made Sam so mad. What was wrong with Aubrey? What kind of person acted like that?

Sam mentally flipped through the names of

everyone she thought could be the bully. "Have you seen Billy Costiff lately?"

Nikki glanced around. "He hasn't said anything since, well, in a while, and he's not supposed to follow me anymore ..."

"But?"

"But I turn corners, and there he is. Only he isn't smiling at me like before."

"What's he doing now?"

"Glaring at me. Throwing mean looks my way." Nikki shuddered. "I know what they mean now when they say *if looks could kill*. It's creepy."

Could his adoration have turned into hatred? Did he hate her now? Enough to send her mean notes, emails, and texts and shove diet bars into her locker?

Where was he last night at 6:44?

"Do you know if he takes EAST?"

Nikki's expression went slack. "Do you think Billy is the bully?"

Sam shrugged. "I'm not ruling anyone out at this point."

"It can't be him. I had to report him for practically stalking me because he had a crush on me."

"And that made him mad, right? You just told me he's been giving you the stink eye."

"But mad enough to be so cruel?"

Sam shrugged. "Maybe he thought you were cruel to reject his attention."

Nikki swallowed loudly. "I didn't think of it that way. His following me around had just gotten to the point where it was a little scary."

"Oh, I'm not saying reporting him was wrong — I totally think you did the right thing. I'm just saying in his mind, he might have thought you two were going to be together and when he was told to back off, it hurt his feelings and made him angry."

"So what do I do?" Nikki stared at the classroom door as if Billy would bust through any moment and torment her.

"Nothing. I'll try to find out if he even takes EAST."

"Thanks, Sam. It means a lot that you're helping me." Nikki turned to look at the editor's desk.

Ms. Pape was gone. Aubrey stood with her clipboard against her chest, staring at Nikki and Sam.

She did *not* look happy.

"I need to go." Nikki headed toward Aubrey, then glanced over her shoulder. "Remember, Sam, don't you dare let anyone know about me."

Sam would do her best to keep Nikki's identity a secret because that's what responsible reporters did. But that didn't mean she couldn't poke around.

And write an article that would hopefully make the bully nervous enough to make a mistake.

CHAPTER ELEVEN

… It's appalling to think someone would use school property to bully someone else. How low can you get?

What do YOU think? Do you think if a student uses a school computer to commit a form of cyber-bullying, they should be expelled? Sound off, Senators. Leave a comment with your thoughts. ~ Sam Sanderson, reporting

"I can *not* believe you wrote an article about this without reporting it." Ms. Pape walked quickly alongside Sam on their way to Mrs. Trees' office.

Thunder rumbled on the dark Thursday morning. Drought-like conditions had settled over Little Rock for weeks, and today of all days, severe weather was forecasted. Of course. Made perfect sense to Sam. Storms seemed to rain on her whenever she was on the edge of uncovering a great story.

"Mrs. Trees called me while she was driving. She's furious. I don't blame her, Sam. You went too far on this one. When it has to do with misuse of school property, you should never write about that until you've reported it to the office." Ms. Pape opened the back door to the office and led Sam inside.

Even the air conditioner was silent as they headed to the principal's office.

"Ms. Pape, I don't have any documented proof."

She spun to face Sam. "Then you shouldn't have written it. That shows sloppy reporting. I'm beyond disappointed in you."

"I *know* it's true."

"Then you do have proof?"

Sam nodded. "Just not that I can share."

Ms. Pape gritted her teeth and shook her head. She pointed at the chair in front of Mrs. Trees' desk. "Sit right there. I'll be back." She left, shutting the door behind her.

Sam couldn't sit. Every muscle in her body felt like doing jumping jacks. She paced in front of the principal's desk.

Mrs. Trees' computer monitor was off center, so Sam could see the tabs she had open. She leaned a little closer to read. One of the open ones was titled *Media Center passcodes* and another one was *EAST class rosters*. Sam glanced at the closed office door. The principal had to know the only two areas where students could access the Internet were the media center and EAST.

Sam held her breath, chewing her bottom lip. Dare she?

She cracked open the office door just a hair and peeked outside. Nobody was around. She shut the door as quietly as she could.

Yes, it was wrong to break into the principal's computer, but the tab was already open. That wasn't really breaking into anything if it was already right there, right? Just sitting there, begging to be looked at.

She looked at the door again. If she did this, she needed to do it now. She'd be in serious trouble if she got caught.

This is wrong.

Funny how her conscience sounded like Makayla's voice.

It was now or never!

Sam leaned over the desk and grabbed the mouse. She brought the *EAST class rosters* tab full screen. She glanced over her shoulder to the door, then back to the page. She began scrolling, looking for names of her possible suspects.

Billy Costiff was in the EAST lab for first period.

Felicia Adams took EAST in third period.

Sam heard voices in the hall. She only had one more name to check. She scrolled down. Yes! Melanie Olson had EAST for fifth period.

Footsteps in the hall.

What about Aubrey? Sam didn't talk to her enough to know if she took EAST or not. She scrolled back up the list.

"Where is Ms. Pape?" Mrs. Trees' voice was muffled, but Sam could tell the principal was just out in the hall on the other side of the door.

Aubrey was in EAST!

She reduced the tab down to the bottom of the screen, returned the mouse to its pad, then straightened.

"Sit down, Samantha." Mrs. Trees marched into her office with Ms. Pape on her heels.

Sam sat, pushing as far back into the chair as she could. She curled her hands into balls on her lap.

Mrs. Trees sat down, dug her elbows into the desk, and laced her fingers. "I'm very disappointed in you."

"I'm sorry." Sam swallowed. Again. Could they hear her heart pounding? As hard as it beat against her chest, they had to.

"You imply in your article that a student used school property — a computer — to perpetrate an illegal act. Is that what you meant to do?"

Sam nodded.

"You must have proof of this, correct? With your mother being who she is, surely you're a responsible enough reporter that you would verify such a fact."

This was going to be ugly. Sam nodded. Slowly. Deliberately.

"What, exactly, is this proof?" Mrs. Trees spoke through white-lined lips. "Why don't you tell me how you came to learn this?" She was really going to hate where this would end.

So would Sam, probably. "Someone received an email that contained information that would definitely fall under the definition of bullying." She'd checked on that last night using an Arkansas legal website.

"Who received the email?" Ms. Pape asked.

"I can't tell you." Sam tightened her fists until her nails dug into her palms.

"But you saw it? Yourself?" Mrs. Trees asked.

Sam nodded, slowly. Were they trying to trip her up?

"I see." Mrs. Trees dropped her hands to the desk and grabbed a pen. She pressed the end. *Click!* "How do you know the email originated from the school?"

Click! Click!

Sam licked her lips. "A source was able to trace the IP address back to the school."

"Where at the school? The front desk? The media center? My office?" Mrs. Trees waved her pen at her monitor.

Click! Click! Click!

Guilty heat crept up the back of Sam's neck. "According to the trace, the email originated from one of the computers in the EAST lab."

Click!

"And you have proof of this trace?"

Sam nodded.

Click! Click!

"I'd like to see that, please."

"I can't."

The pen hit the desk. "Excuse me?"

Sam's leg muscles bunched. "I can't reveal my sources."

The principal's eyes narrowed into little slits under her drawn-on eyebrows.

Sam scooted to the edge of the chair. "I'm sorry, Mrs. Trees, I really am, but I can't tell you."

"You can't tell me who received this alleged email or who can verify the trace back to one of the computers here on my campus?"

Sam shook her head. "I can't reveal my sources, Mrs. Trees. I'm trying to be a responsible reporter. The information is factual. I've confirmed my allegations. You can take my word for it."

"Take your word?" Mrs. Trees shook her head. "No, Samantha, I don't think I can do that. I'm afraid I must insist you tell me who received the email and who traced its origins."

"I'm sorry. I can't tell you either."

"Can't or won't?" No softness lined even a single wrinkle in the principal's face.

"I can't reveal my sources, Mrs. Trees. No one would ever talk to me again if I did. It's critical to my career for people to know that if I say I won't use their name, then I won't."

"Your *career*?" Mrs. Trees flashed Sam a humorless smile. "At this point, Samantha, I would think you'd be more worried about not getting suspended than a career at least half a decade in the future."

Suspended? Sam's mouth went totally dry.

"At least show us the email, Sam," Ms. Pape all but begged. "We can have someone run a trace as your source did. It's a way for us to verify the proof."

Sam appreciated the paper's teacher-sponsor's trying to help. "I can't. The person was adamant that they not be revealed."

Mrs. Trees pulled out a piece of paper and began writing. "If you won't tell us, you've given me no other choice."

Sam stared at the paper, heat flooding her face and pulse ringing in her ears. "You're suspending me?"

Mrs. Trees signed the form, pulled off the top copy, and passed it across the desk to Sam. "Beginning tomorrow."

Air wouldn't enter her lungs. Sam couldn't focus on the writing. "For how long?"

"That depends on you."

"What?"

"You can return as soon as you like. As soon as you're ready to tell us the truth."

Sam found her voice and her backbone. She jumped to her feet. "You can't do this, Mrs. Trees."

"I can. The student handbook that you signed at the beginning of the year states that even if you don't agree with the rules of this school and this school district, you must adhere to them." Mrs. Trees stood as well. "It is in the interest of student safety that you reveal this information. To not do so puts other students at risk."

Sam opened her mouth to argue, then decided not to. She was, after all, just a kid.

"You may go back to class." Mrs. Trees sat back down. "For today."

Ms. Pape stayed put.

Sam reached for the door knob.

"And Sam?"

She glanced back to Mrs. Trees. "Yes, ma'am?"

"If you decide to reconsider your decision during the course of the school day today, come see me. I'd hate for this suspension to cause you to lose your spot on the cheer squad." She glanced at Ms. Pape. "Or your place on the school paper."

This could not be happening!

"Can she do that?" Makayla asked in third period. "Isn't it like coercion or something, which is illegal?"

Sam rubbed the back of her neck. She was pretty

sure there were measures in place to protect all jour-
nalists, even those in middle school, against pressure
to force them to reveal their sources. She'd certainly
research that tonight. "She sure acts like she can do it."

"She's just trying to scare you, right?" Makayla's deep
brown eyes were wide. "She's just bluffing, hoping you'll
come forward by the end of the day."

"I don't know. I hope she isn't."

"What are you going to do?"

Sam grinned. "Don't worry, Mac. I'm not going to
drag you into this mess."

"Thanks. I mean, I don't want you to get in trouble
…"

"It's not your fault, Mac. You practically begged me
to tell Mrs. Trees yesterday. Even on the phone last
night, you told me to tell her. I just wanted to write the
scoop." Which may not only have cost her the editor
position next year, but also cost her place on the cheer
squad. She blinked back the tears starting to burn her
eyes. "I should have listened."

Makayla nodded. "My mother will have a hissy fit
if she finds out. She's already acting all crazy over my
grades and that whole homeschooling spell she went
through last month. But I don't want to make you take
the fall for all of this. I especially don't want you to get
suspended."

Sam swallowed. Her father was going to kill her.

Maybe Mom would know if what Mrs. Trees was doing was legal.

Just another reason Mom shouldn't leave. Sam needed her here. Needed her help. Her advice. Her support. Without it, there was the very good chance Dad was going to go ape crazy. He'd ground her at the very least. As a cop, he was a stickler for following rules.

Makayla grabbed Sam's hand and squeezed. "I have karate after school, but call me when you can and let me know what's going on."

"If I'm not grounded." She had to shake this off. Sam smiled at Makayla and let out a long breath. "But I did find out something else."

"What?"

"Billy Costiff, Melanie Olson, Felicia Adams, and Aubrey all take EAST, so all of them would have logins to the computers."

Makayla glanced at the keyboarding teacher, Mrs. Forge. Their teacher was at least fifty years old. Her short, gray hair looked like she'd been electrocuted because it stuck out all over her head. And those glasses she wore? They made her eyes look bigger than a big, ole bullfrog's.

"Sam, how do you know that?" Makayla asked.

She grinned. "It's probably best I don't tell you. That way, you can honestly say you have no idea. Just in case you're ever asked or anything."

Makayla shook her head. "Do you really think Aubrey is a suspect?"

"With the way she's been treating Nikki, I wouldn't put anything past her."

"Jealousy is a very strong emotion."

Sam shrugged. "I don't know, Mac. If you were nominated and I wasn't, I'd be so excited and happy for you."

"But being on homecoming court isn't important to you. It is to Aubrey."

Sam just couldn't wrap her mind around how being popular was so important. Yet, Makayla was right that being popular was very important to Aubrey. "Well, everybody's a suspect right now."

And would be until Sam could check out their alibis. She'd start on that tonight. Unless her dad killed her first.

CHAPTER TWELVE

God, I got myself into this mess, but please, please, please help me.

Sam had held out all through the ride home from school with Mom, making dinner with her, and having Dad help with some math homework. Now, as the three of them sat silently around the table eating, Sam knew she couldn't put it off any longer.

"Mom, Dad ..." The tension was still so thick.

Both of them looked up from their plates.

No easy way to say it. Might as well just get it out there, then try to soften the blow with an explanation. "I, um, got suspended today." She set the suspension form on the table between them. "It starts tomorrow."

"What?" Dad's face went red as Mom snatched up the form.

"Suspension for violation of rule 102, defiant behavior," Mom read Mrs. Trees' notes. "And for failure to report knowledge of violation of rule 314, unauthorized accessing or attempting to access computer files, and failure to report knowledge of violation of rule 306, bullying." Mom laid down the paper. "What's going on?"

Dad grabbed the form before she could say anything. "It doesn't say how many days you're suspended."

"Let me explain." And as carefully as she could, she told them everything. When she had finished, she gulped down the rest of her tea.

"She can't do that!" Mom warped into full Freedom-of-the-Press-defender mode. "Unless this principal utilizes legal channels, she lacks the authority to force any student journalist to reveal confidential information."

"Your principal said you were suspended until you told her who was being bullied and who traced the email origin back to the school's computers?" Dad asked.

"This is classic violation of so many rights that I don't even know where to begin." Mom stood and paced, gripping her constant-companion-cell-phone and reading from it. "Without a court-issued subpoena ordering disclosure, you, Sam, are protected by the First Amendment or Arkansas state law from having to disclose your sources, and you are under no obligation to respond to demands." Even wearing yoga pants and socks, Mom looked ready to do battle. "And for her to mention the possibility of losing your place on cheer squad because of this suspension ... that's nothing more than intimidation."

"Let's back up a minute," Dad said. "Is this person who got the email the same person you talked to me about being bullied?"

Sam nodded.

"So they've gotten notes at their home, texts, something put in their locker, and now an email?"

Again she nodded.

"Sam, I told you bullies don't stop. This proves my point. This bully is getting more aggressive. You need to tell me who this person is so I can talk with her parents and intervene before it's too late."

Mom spun and stared at Dad with wide, wide eyes. "What? You're just as bad as the principal, Charles. She isn't at liberty to tell you who it is. The person has told Sam to keep her name out of it. Sam has to respect her wishes."

Dad stood, carrying his plate to the sink, then leaned against the counter and stared at his wife. "Joy, this isn't just about protecting a source, this is about protecting a kid. You've read enough to know that when bullies become more and more aggressive, as this one clearly is, violence can easily follow. I'm trying to keep a kid safe."

Mom shook her head as Sam carried her and Mom's plates to the sink. "But it *is* about protecting a source. This girl specifically told Sam to keep her name out of it. If Sam reveals her identity, she's betrayed the girl's trust. The girl will be furious, and Sam's reputation as being trustworthy will be shot."

Way to go, Mom!

"Which is more important: keeping her safe, or keeping her identity as secret?" Dad pushed off the counter and raised his voice. "The two are exclusive of each other. You can't have both. So it comes down to is it more important for this girl to be safe but upset, or for Sam to keep her secret, even if it means harm comes to the girl?"

Tears burned Sam's eyes. Both Mom and Dad had valid points, but what was worse was that they were arguing. Over her. Sam couldn't take it anymore. "I'm sorry. Please stop fighting."

Mom and Dad went silent, turning to stare at her.

"I'm sorry I got suspended. I'm sorry I can't tell who she is, but I'll try to get her to let me tell you at least, Dad. Her parents know and think the bully will move on to someone else soon. I'm sorry I can't tell who traced the IP address." Sam's voice cracked. "Just please, please quit arguing."

"Oh, my sweet girl, I'm sorry." Mom crossed the room and pulled Sam into a hug. "We aren't mad at you. We're not fighting. We're just debating."

Sam pulled away, swiping at the tears that had escaped. "No, Mom, y'all aren't debating. You two are arguing. Y'all have been arguing ever since you got home. I feel like I'm supposed to pick sides, but I can't. I love you both."

Dad turned Sam into his own hug. "Sweetheart, we love you, too. I'm sorry if you feel like you have to pick sides. Neither of us would ever put you in such a position. Not on purpose. I'm sorry. Just know that your mother and I are praying about this issue. Together."

"I didn't even realize we'd put so much pressure on you," Mom said. "I'm sorry, my sweet girl."

"It's not just this." Sam wiped her eyes. Why couldn't she stop crying? "I don't want you to go for six months, Mom, but I don't want you to stay because me or Dad guilt you into it because then, later on, you'd resent us for holding you back from this great opportunity. I want you to stay, but I want you to go, too." She wiped her nose on her sleeve. "But I'm really glad you're praying about it together. That makes me feel a lot better."

Sam took another step back. "And on this, I'm sorry Mrs. Trees suspended me. I don't think she should be able to, but I don't know since she cited rules and stuff. Either way, I can't tell anyone who it is because I promised I wouldn't." She met Dad's stare. "You've always told me that a person is only as good as their word. I can't break that. At least, not yet. I don't think she's in danger, and neither does she or her parents."

"Sam, bullies can escalate their methods so quickly — " Dad started.

"I understand what you're saying, Dad, which is why I'm trying to help her figure out who the bully is."

Dad shook his head. "Which might very well put you in the bully's crosshairs, too, Sam. Did you stop to consider that?"

No, she hadn't. "I don't think that's going to be a problem, but if it were, at least then I would have evidence I could give you and Mrs. Trees."

Dad went back to the suspension form and scanned it. "This part: for failure to report knowledge of violation of rule 314, unauthorized accessing or attempting to access computer files — you can ask whoever did the tracing to let you give the principal that information, though."

Sam shook her head. No matter what, she would not pull Makayla into this. "I'm sorry, but I can't."

Mom's gaze locked with Sam's. She knew Makayla was a computer whiz and that whenever Sam needed technical information, Mac would supply it.

"Why not?" Dad frowned. "You didn't do anything wrong to get the information, did you? Did the person access computer files of the school's computers?"

"No, sir." She licked her lips. Makayla hadn't broken any laws or rules to trace the information, but guilt strangled Sam as she remembered looking up the EAST students on Mrs. Trees' computer. That was certainly a violation of rule 314.

"If you got the information through legitimate

avenues, why can't you provide that tracing information?" Dad asked.

"Because I can't." She wouldn't tell on Makayla. Her mom would seriously freak out. Probably pull her out of Robinson and home school her. No, Sam couldn't put Mac in such a position, and she knew Mom wouldn't say anything.

Dad sighed. Long. Loudly.

"I'm sorry, Dad. I really am. I'd tell you if I could."

"I understand why your principal is so frustrated," Dad groaned.

"Being frustrated isn't a license to suspend someone covered under the Arkansas shield law," Mom said.

"What, exactly, is the shield law?" Dad asked.

Mom lifted her ever-present iPhone and read. *"Any editor, reporter, or other writer for any newspaper, periodical, or radio station is protected from revealing his or her sources unless the party seeking disclosure can show that the article was written in bad faith, with malice, and not in the interest of the public welfare."*

Dad cocked his head to the side. "I don't think Sam wrote with malice or bad faith, and exposing bullying for the crime it is, well, that's certainly public interest. Especially to middle school students."

"Of course not," Mom said. She ran a finger over her phone's touch screen to scroll. "The shield law does not specify whether the source must be promised confidentiality to be protected. In 1978, the Arkansas Supreme

Court held that the state's shield law applied to both civil and criminal proceedings. The court also stated that even where the bad faith/malice requirement is met, the party seeking disclosure should also make a *reasonable effort* to obtain the information by alternative means."

"What does that mean?" Sam asked.

"Did your principal try to find out who was being bullied by any other means than asking you?" Mom asked.

Sam shook her head.

"Did she have anybody check out those computers in the EAST lab to see if a breach was detected?"

Again Sam shook her head. "Not that I know about."

Mom looked at Dad. "I'm betting she made no other effort, aside from questioning our daughter, to obtain any of this information, which puts her actions against Sam in direct violation of the shield law."

He nodded.

Mom smiled at Dad. He smiled back at her. They both wore those goofy looks like when they cuddled on the couch. Gross.

Sam shuddered before they turned totally mushy. "What does that mean?"

"It means you're going to school tomorrow," Mom said. "I'll be taking you and will meet with your principal first thing."

The fun was about to begin.

● ● ●

"Sorry I missed your call." Sam leaned against her headboard and rubbed Chewy's belly. "I was having a serious discussion with my parents," she said into her iPhone.

"About getting suspended?" Nikki asked.

"Yeah. Dad flipped, but it's okay now." Sam stopped petting her dog and drew her knees to her chest. "You heard about it?"

"Yeah. Listen, I wanted to thank you for not giving my name to Mrs. Trees. Especially since she suspended you for not telling. My mom would be mortified if my name was brought into the mess and if it hurt my chances at homecoming queen."

That would be why Mrs. Cole would be mortified? Not that someone was bullying her daughter? Sam licked her lips. "It worked out. Mom says she can't suspend me, so she's bringing me to school tomorrow and will talk to Mrs. Trees."

"I'd love to hear that conversation," Nikki said.

Remembering the look in her mom's eyes when she went all defender-of-Freedom-of-the-Press mode, Sam laughed. "I don't know that I want to be there. It probably won't be pretty. Mom says all reporters, even school paper reporters, are covered under the state shield law. I'm sure she plans to inform Mrs. Trees all about that."

Nikki chuckled, too. "Your mom's a famous journalist, so I bet she'll give Mrs. Trees an earful."

"I'm sure. We'll know how it goes if they let me stay in school."

"I hadn't planned on telling you this, but, well, you've more than proved you won't tell."

"What?" Sam sat upright in the bed fast enough that Chewy startled, then jumped to the floor.

"When I got home from school today and checked the mail, I had a package from Amazon. I hadn't ordered anything, so I was pretty excited. When I opened the box, it was a bottle of diet pills." Nikki sniffed over the connection. "I can assure you that I didn't order them."

OhMyGummyBears! "Did you look at the packing slip?"

"I did. It has my mom's name on it." Nikki sniffed again. "You don't think my mom ordered them for me, do you?"

Sam's instinct was to say no, but she didn't know Mrs. Cole that well. "I wouldn't think she would. Not without telling you anyway."

"I didn't think so either, so I threw the pills and box away."

What? Destroying evidence? "Did you throw away the packing slip, too?" *Please say no.*

"Well, yes."

Sam swallowed the desire to scream. "Can you get it back? The packing slip at least?"

"It's in the garbage can outside."

"Can you get it?"

Nikki sighed. "Maybe. Depends on if Jefferson carried out the trash today like he was supposed to. If he did, there's no way I'm going to dig through all that stuff. It's nasty."

"If you can, get the packing slip and bring it to school tomorrow. If I'm still there by last period, I'll get it and see if I can do some searching." Sam struggled to keep her voice even. This could be a huge break. When someone ordered something from Amazon, they had to pay for it, so it had to go to someone's account.

"I'll try. If I can, I'll bring it." Nikki coughed. "Do you think your mom will get Mrs. Trees to forget about the suspension?"

"I don't know." Mom was sure adamant that Mrs. Trees couldn't suspend her. "I think so."

"Good. I hope you aren't. Then I'd feel really bad."

No time for more guilt trips. "Hey, did you get any homecoming queen campaign posters put up?"

"I did. About ten, but four mysteriously disappeared. I reported that to Mrs. Creegle."

Sam remembered what Makayla had overheard Mrs. Trees say to Felicia. "Do you know Felicia Adams personally?"

"Not really, why?"

"No reason." No point in making Nikki worried about someone else not liking her if Felicia didn't turn out to be the bully.

"Hey, listen, my mom's hollering for me to help Jefferson with his homework before our dad comes by to check on us. And before you ask, I'm *not* telling my parents about the diet pills. If Mom did order them, Dad will get mad, and they've been getting along really well lately, so I don't want to say anything that could change that."

"Okay, I understand. Don't forget about the packing slip," Sam said.

"I won't. And thanks again, Sam, for having my back."

Sam hung up the phone. How long would she be able to keep it all a secret if Mom couldn't talk Mrs. Trees out of the suspension? If she missed ten days a semester, she wouldn't pass. She couldn't do seventh grade again. It'd be part of her permanent record, and she'd never get the Mizzou scholarship.

God, please help me.

CHAPTER THIRTEEN

Knots tightened in Sam's stomach.

She glanced at Mrs. Darrington, who didn't even look up from her desk. Kids talked loudly as they passed the door on their way to class. The bell had rung a few minutes ago, and according to the clock on the wall in the school office, the tardy bell would sound in twenty-one seconds.

Twenty.

Nineteen.

Sam glanced down the hall toward Mrs. Trees' office. Mom had been in there for at least fifteen minutes. Right after Mom had gone in there, Mrs. Shine had rushed in. Was that a good sign or not?

Brring!

She tapped her backpack sitting on the floor

between her feet with her toes and let out a slow breath. Her cheer practice clothes were inside it. Would she get kicked off the cheer team before today was over? She hoped not. She really loved cheer.

The office door opened and several students filed inside, all jockeying for the computer on the front desk to get their tardy pass.

Melanie Olson was in the back of the line. She gave a little nod to Sam.

Sam smiled back, bigger than she normally would.

A bit hesitantly, Melanie moved closer. "What're you in here for?"

"I might be suspended."

"That's right. I heard that yesterday afternoon."

"Yeah." Sam watched two kids tear off their passes and leave. Only three were in line before Melanie. "You late because you got hung up at your locker?" She needed to figure out how to work Nikki into the conversation, and quickly.

Melanie frowned. "No. Traffic." She hoisted her backpack to her shoulder. "We had to move to an apartment, and the district hasn't updated the bus route for us yet, so Mom's having to drop me off on her way to work. I've been late four times already this semester."

"I'm sorry."

"Not your fault. If my dad hadn't lost his job, none of this would be happening."

Another student grabbed her pass and left.

"I'm sorry your dad lost his job. He worked at the Hewlett Packard plant in Conway, right?" She didn't mean to be blunt, but she was running out of time.

"Yeah, until Mrs. Cole fired him." Melanie shook her head. "It's not fair that Mrs. Cole still has her job and is able to keep living in her pretty house with Nikki and Jefferson, but my dad got laid off after almost ten years, and we have to move to an apartment."

"It's not her fault, Melanie. Mrs. Cole didn't make the decision."

Melanie snorted. "Think that all you want, but she doesn't seem too torn up about wrecking everyone's lives. Like five hundred lives."

The girl in front of Melanie tore off her pass and headed out the door. Melanie scanned her student ID badge, then clicked on the big TARDY button. Her pass printed out. "See you later," she told Sam as she headed out the door.

Maybe Melanie was more of a suspect than Sam had first considered.

The door to the office opened, and Dad and his new partner, Buster Roscoe, strode. Dad did *not* look happy to see her.

Mrs. Darrington shot to her feet. "May I help you?" Her eyes were drawn to Buster with his smooth black skin, his shiny bald head, and dark eyes. There was something about him that made people tell him their deepest, darkest secrets. At least that's what Dad said.

"We're Detectives Sanderson and Roscoe, here to see Mrs. Trees," Dad said. "She's expecting us."

What? She'd called the police? Sam's anxiousness flipped into overdrive.

"Oh, about the break-in. Of course. Let me escort you to her office." Mrs. Darrington made a motion to come from behind the counter.

"It's okay. I know the way." Dad led Detective Roscoe down the hallway, not even looking back at Sam.

Mrs. Darrington watched them leave, then met Sam's gaze. "Isn't that your dad?"

"Yes, ma'am."

She made a harrumphing sound before going back to her desk.

Break-in? What was going on?

"Sam," Mom said.

Sam lifted her backpack and met her mom in the hallway. "What's going on?"

"You aren't suspended, but you'll most likely be questioned by your father in a few moments."

"What?" Sam's heart skipped a beat. "Questioned?"

"I can't explain more just yet, but Mrs. Trees asks that you just sit tight for a few minutes." Mom gave her a quick hug. "It's going to be okay. I have to run. I have a meeting with Pastor Patterson. I'll pick you up after cheer practice." She planted a quick kiss on Sam's cheek, then headed out the door.

Sam slumped back onto the bench, still clutching

her backpack strap. She couldn't imagine what on earth Dad would need to question her about. Nothing made sense. At least she wasn't kicked off cheer squad.

She had missed being able to talk to Makayla this morning because Mom had made her come sit in the office and wait while she talked with Mrs. Trees. At least they'd talked on the phone last night. Makayla hated that Sam was in the hot seat, and had offered a possible solution: give them the bogus address the email had been sent from. That would give them some place to start. Sam hadn't volunteered that. Maybe, if Mom hadn't been able to talk Mrs. Trees into dismissing the suspension, she would've offered that up.

The intercom buzzed. Mrs. Darrington answered it and spoke into the receiver quietly before replacing it to its cradle. "Sam, they want you in Mrs. Trees' office."

Sam stood on wobbly knees and made her way down the hall. It felt like she was headed to the guillotines they'd studied in history earlier in September. The floor pulled at her feet, slowing every single step.

Finally outside Mrs. Trees' office, she knocked softly on the door.

"Come in," Mrs. Trees' voice practically boomed.

She nudged the door open.

"Come in, Sam, and have a seat." Mrs. Trees waved at the empty chair beside Detective Roscoe.

Dad stood closer to the corner, leaning against the wall with his arms crossed over his chest. He didn't make eye contact with Sam or acknowledge her in any way.

"I'm sure your mother informed you that I have graciously reconsidered your suspension," the principal said.

Sam nodded. *Graciously reconsidered?* More likely that Mom had called her out, and Mrs. Trees had no choice but to dismiss the suspension, but if she wanted to save face ... whatever.

"What you're here for now is a different matter."

Sam held her breath, waiting.

"Last night or early this morning, the school's EAST lab was broken into."

Sam gasped.

Mrs. Trees continued. "Three computers were stolen."

"No way!" So many of the school's business partners had helped with raising the funds for the newer computers.

"After informing the police about your knowledge of some unknown party breaking into the EAST lab to send an email on Tuesday evening, they were most interested in questioning you." Mrs. Trees smiled, but it wasn't a nice kind of smile. More like a smirk.

Sam didn't like it. "I don't know who broke in to send the email."

"Samantha," Detective Roscoe began.

"It's just Sam."

He smiled, revealing a row of perfectly straight and obnoxiously white teeth. "Sam. We understand you don't know the person's identity, but we need to know everything you know so we can investigate this theft to the best of our abilities."

Oh, he was good, Sam would give him that. "I don't know anything."

Dad pushed off the wall and sat on the edge of Mrs. Trees' desk. "What about the email you traced back to having been sent from one of these computers?"

"I can't give you that. You know this." That was what was most frustrating — Dad knew she couldn't tell him. They'd discussed this to the point of insanity last night.

"Can you tell us anything about the email? Maybe just what was written? There might be something we can go off by knowing how something was worded," Detective Roscoe said.

That was something she hadn't considered. Sam licked her lips. She mentally went over the email's content. The part about being nominated for homecoming court would let them know it was one of six people. No way would Nikki let her give them that. Sam couldn't tell them everything. Not after having just proved her word was good.

But she could tell them some of what was in the email. "Some of it, I can't share with you."

"Some of it you can?" Detective Roscoe asked.

She nodded. Sam pulled a spiral notebook from her

backpack. She grabbed the pen off Mrs. Tree's desk and wrote: "You are so fat. Ugly. You … as a joke. Everybody knows that but you. Now you are the joke." She handed the paper to Detective Roscoe. "I didn't put in the part that I can't share with you."

"Thank you, Sam." His voice was soft, soothing. He scanned the paper, then handed it to Dad before returning his attention back to her. "Are you sure this is exactly how it was worded in the original email?"

She nodded. "Positive. I have a freakish memory for stuff like this." She smiled and cut her eyes to the principal, then back to him. "Comes in handy when studying for tests."

Detective Roscoe flashed that bright smile of his again. "I would imagine it does."

With that smile, Sam could easily imagine suspects spilling their guts to him.

"Is there anything else you can tell us about the email?"

Sam remembered what Makayla had told her last night on the phone. "The email address it came from."

Dad handed the paper back to his partner and faced Sam with his bulldog look. "You couldn't have told me this last night? Or your principal yesterday?"

She tried to swallow, but the boulder caught in the back of her throat. "I couldn't."

"But you can today?" Dad's face grew redder and redder.

"What's the email address?" Detective Roscoe asked in a soft and even tone.

"*truthtelr*-at-*gmail*-dot-*com*." She spelled it out for him.

He jotted it on the bottom of her sheet. "Anything else?" His smile was blinding and more annoying now.

"That's it. That's all I can tell you."

Detective Roscoe folded the sheet and slipped it in the front pocket of his shirt. "This is a good start. Thank you, Sam."

She nodded.

"Sam, I'll appeal to you again to at least tell the counselor who is being bullied," Dad said. "As I've explained, these situations usually escalate."

"I'll keep encouraging the person to visit Mrs. Creegle."

"Our Pathfinders is a great counseling program here. Mrs. Creegle will be happy to assist your friend in signing up," Mrs. Trees said, all smiles.

"I'll remind her."

"Sam," Dad said in a low voice, drawing her attention. "If you have any information about the break-in . . ."

"I don't. I promise. I learned about it when I came in here."

"Okay. But if you hear anything, you need to let the office know, or me," Dad's tone left no doubt that it was an order and not a request.

"You may go to class, Samantha." Mrs. Trees handed her a pass. It was marked as an excused tardy.

She grabbed her backpack and hurried out of the office before they changed their minds and asked her more questions. She all but ran up the stairs of both ramps before stopping at her locker. Sam quickly hung up her backpack with her practice clothes inside and swapped out books. She slammed the locker shut and headed to English class.

It was hard to pay attention in classes all day as talk floated around campus about the stolen computers. Dad and Detective Roscoe had called in a Crime Scene Unit, so the EAST lab was closed off to everyone all day. EAST classes were held in the media center, where the EAST students were questioned by Dad and his partner.

Lunch had been quite loud with everyone talking over one another. Sam saw Nikki sitting across the cafeteria close to Aubrey. She waited until Aubrey had gone back to the food counter for a napkin, then rushed to Nikki. "Did you get the shipping label?"

Nikki shot a quick look at the counter where Aubrey was chatting with Paul Moore. Nikki pulled out a crumbled piece of paper and handed it to Sam. "Here."

Sam took the label and pushed it into her pocket before heading back to her seat. Aubrey stared hard at Sam as she returned to her seat close to Nikki.

Sitting down, Sam showed Makayla the packing slip. "Look ... the order was in Nikki's mom's name."

"Surely her mother wouldn't have ordered diet pills for her. All of those are dangerous for teenagers," Makayla said.

"I bet someone used her account." Sam stared at the label. "Would it be hard to hack into someone's Amazon account?"

"Depends. From an outside system? They'd have to be better than whoever sent Nikki the email. But from a computer where Mrs. Cole had logged into her account? It could be done fairly easy. Even for an amateur."

"I wonder if Mrs. Cole has logged in on her work computer." Sam thought aloud.

Makayla let out a little laugh. "I'm sure she has. A recent study reported that over seventy-three percent of employees have used their workplace computer to order something non-work related."

Sam shook her head. "You and your studies."

Makayla laughed as lunch drew to an end. Sam gave her bestie a hug before heading back to class. She still had two more classes to suffer through until newspaper. For the first time in her life, she dreaded going to the Senator Speak classroom. What if Ms. Pape kicked her off the newspaper? Surely Mom had stressed to Mrs. Trees that wasn't an alternative to the suspension.

By the time the bell rang for last period, the rumor

was that someone in EAST had stolen the computers. Sam went into the newsroom, her stomach tightening again.

Aubrey stood in the front of the class. "I guess everyone's heard by now about the break-in at our school last night."

Murmurs went around the room.

"While Samantha's father is on the case, Ms. Pape and I feel we should give the story to someone else. This will also allow *Samantha* to continue her series on bullying." Aubrey shot Sam one of her snarky smiles.

Sam started to debate, but caught the look on Ms. Pape's face. It was obvious arguing would be futile, so instead, she just opened the notes section on her iPad to look at her notes on bullying.

"I'm going to assign Nikki the story about the break-in and theft," Aubrey announced.

CHAPTER FOURTEEN

"Hey," Bella said to the group at large as she stretched before cheer practice. "I asked Luke Jensen to escort me. We've been friends since we were babies, since his mom and mine were college roommates."

Just the mention of Luke's name perked up Sam's interest. Luke Jensen was, in Sam's humble opinion, the cutest boy in seventh grade with his sandy blond, wavy hair and eyes that reminded Sam of dark chocolate. They'd gone to school together since kindergarten, but lately, every time she got near him, Sam's mind refused to remember how to speak. It was like her tongue turned to stone, and she could only grunt and nod like an idiot.

"What are you talking about?" Sam asked.

"All the homecoming court girls have to have a guy escort them at the pep rally. The fathers will be the escorts onto the field homecoming night, but Mrs. Trees doesn't want anybody to have to miss work to come to the pep rally, so we have to ask a guy at school." Bella answered. "Most of us asked guys who are our friends so it wouldn't be so weird."

"I heard Lana asked Jared from newspaper staff," Kate replied. "They've been friends for a long time, too."

"Not me. I actually invited someone I like who I think is epic," Remy said.

"Who?" Frannie asked.

"Kevin Haynes." Remy smiled and widened her eyes. "Not only is he the quarterback and president of the student council, he's also captain of the debate team, and leader of the Alpha gifted program."

As if everybody didn't know. Especially the cheerleaders, since they cheered for him every game.

Sam bit her lip. Everybody knew Aubrey had a huge crush on Kevin Haynes. She would flip out when she learned he'd be escorting Remy. Just another reason Aubrey had to be angry for not being nominated.

"I asked someone I've had a crush on for a while," Lin almost whispered. "He doesn't know, but I thought asking him might lead to an opportunity to let him know."

"Who?" Frannie asked.

"Tam." Lin's cheeks went red as Rudolph's nose.

"Get out!" Remy gave Lin a soft shove. "Y'all would totally make a cute couple. He has some serious eyes."

"You really think so?"

Remy nodded. "Oh, yeah."

"He's super sweet, too," Sam joined the conversation. "Offered to help me with lots of the anti-bullying campaigns."

Lin smiled, still blushing. "What about you, Frannie?"

"Oh, I asked Marcus."

"Do you like him?" Kate asked.

Frannie shrugged, but her cheeks turned a little pink, too. "Maybe. He's really quiet, but he's sweet once you get to know him."

"Has anybody heard who Nikki asked?" Kate asked.

Remy nodded. "I have third period with her. She asked Thomas Murphy. I don't think they're lifelong buds, so maybe she likes him. He seemed pretty excited, too."

"Oh, they'd make a cute couple, too," Frannie said.

Sam swallowed. Felicia Adams would be royally ticked off when she saw them at the pep rally. Had Nikki unwittingly annoyed her bully even more? Maybe she should have told Nikki who some of her suspects were.

"Okay, girls, enough stretching. Five laps around the gym. Come on." Mrs. Holt blew her whistle.

The girls groaned as they helped one another up and began to jog. The practice would be brutal since they didn't have a game tonight. Sam always hated the away-game weeks because Mrs. Holt felt like they should practice harder since they didn't have to cheer at a game.

Sam felt lucky she hadn't been kicked off the squad, although that had more to do with Mom than blind luck. Mrs. Holt had mentioned to Sam that her mother called earlier and might be a few minutes late picking her up. Sam swallowed the smile. Mom wasn't going to be late — it was just her way of contacting the cheer coach to smooth the way for Sam.

Mom was pretty amazing. If she decided to take the six-month job, Sam would miss her something terrible. For more than one reason.

Celeste hung back to trot alongside Sam. "Hey, what's your dad say about the break-in? I can't believe they stole three computers."

"Dad's not really discussing the case with me."

"Why?"

Sam worked on evening out her breathing so she could jog and talk at the same time, but not slow enough that Mrs. Holt would get angry and think she wasn't running hard enough. "He's just not sharing information. He can't really, I guess."

"I can get that. It's his job and all. Were you upset Aubrey gave the story to Nikki instead of you?" Celeste asked.

"Surprised more than upset." That was the truth. Sam couldn't help but wonder what Aubrey's deal was. She never gave Nikki any of the headliner-type stories. For her to assign this one to Nikki … had Nikki told Aubrey about the email? Did she tell her about tracing it back to EAST lab? It would be just like Aubrey to assign a story to Nikki that could hurt Nikki in some way.

Aubrey was just a vile, horrid person.

"I heard the only things they took were two Mac-Books and one of the older HP all-in-one desktops," Celeste offered.

Sam slowed her pace. "There were three other Mac-Books. I wonder why they'd take the old HP desktop?"

"Dunno. Just what I heard. Come on, we're the last ones running." Celeste gave her a shove and burst ahead.

Sam raced as well. There was no way the HP desktop would bring in near as much money as the MacBooks. Why take them?

But what if selling the computers for money wasn't the motive for the break-in?

Dinner was another tense meal in the Sanderson home.

Sam avoided the subject of the break-in at school. She talked about cheer and the new fan lift pyramid they were working on and hoped to perform next week. Mom asked all the interested parent questions, but Sam could tell she was preoccupied.

Dad, on the other hand, didn't even bother to ask questions. He ate in silence, his gulps of tea the only sound they heard from him.

They'd just finished eating when Mom's cell rang. She glanced at the caller ID. "I have to take this. It's my editor." She headed toward the living room. "Hi, Emily."

As she cleared the table, Sam figured she had nothing to lose. "How's the investigation going, Dad?"

The wet paper towel he had been using to wipe the counters froze. "I can't discuss the case with you, Sam."

"I'm not even assigned the break-in with the paper, Dad. I'm just trying to help."

He didn't answer, just went back to wiping the counters.

"Were you able to find anything on the email?"

Dad sighed. "I'm sure you know the email account was created, the email sent, then the account deleted."

"That's what we thought."

"You could have told me everything last night, Sam." He threw the paper towels in the trash. "You could have given me the content of the email and the sender's address last night. Why didn't you?"

Sam shrugged. "I didn't think about it. I'm sorry. It didn't occur to me."

Dad leaned against the counter. "I know I sometimes come across as the cop and not your dad, but you know how important my job is and when it's connected to your school in some way ... well, my concern for you and the other students can make me seem a little harsh. I don't mean to, but I hope you understand."

"I do. It's just hard for me sometimes, too."

He pulled her into a hug. "I love you, Pumpkin." He kissed the top of her head.

"I love you, too, Daddy."

Stepping back, he cleared his throat. "I'm sorry you didn't get the story for the paper. Because of your principal?"

"I think so, but it's okay. I have some great information for the anti-bullying articles. I'm just a little bummed my article won't be on the blog tomorrow morning. The break-in will be featured instead."

He nodded.

"Dad, something's been bugging me all afternoon. I understand if you can't talk to me about it, but I wanted to share my thoughts on it with you." She dropped onto one of the barstools.

He leaned against the counter. "Go ahead, shoot."

"Do you know how the lab was broken into? I mean, I'm pretty sure they got into the room by the window, but do you have an idea how they got on campus?"

Dad pointed at her. "This is strictly off the record, right? Just a father talking with his daughter, and only her, right?"

She nodded. "Yes, sir."

"The front gates were locked, as were the gates to the entrances."

She nodded. "So they had to get in another way?"

"Either they drove around the gates, but there are no tire tracks in the grass, or they came through by way of the high school." Since the schools were side-by-side and shared the football field and gym, kids were always walking the path between them.

Sam chewed her bottom lip. "Can I give you my theory?"

He nodded. "I'd love to hear it."

She let out a long breath. "Okay. I figured it had to be a kid who broke in to send the email. I mean, if it was an adult, surely they could've found another computer. And why would an adult send such an email to a kid, right?"

"I'm with you."

She smiled and continued. "So I reasoned that the kid goes to our school because they had to have a passcode to get into the computers to send the email. That being the case, the kid wouldn't have a driver's license, so couldn't very well drive to the school, break in to send an email, then drive off."

"Sound reasoning," Dad said.

"So there has to be a way someone who doesn't drive can get onto the property and into the school. With the gates locked, no one can get in from the front."

Dad nodded.

"So, now I have to consider the computers taken. Two MacBooks and one HP. There were other

MacBooks in there. Even some older PC laptops which would have been much easier to steal than a desktop, which makes me think that stealing them wasn't to sell them and make money."

Dad stood up straight. "What's your theory about why the computers were stolen?"

"I think when my article ran about someone having used one of the lab computers to send a bullying email, it made the bully nervous. This person never thought someone would figure that much out. They got so worried that they might have left some kind of evidence of who they were on the computer, so they broke in again, this time to steal the computer they sent the email from." She ran her finger along the edge of the counter. "But they didn't think anyone would figure it out, so they thought by stealing the two MacBooks, the police wouldn't connect the two break-ins."

"What does that tell you about the person?"

Sam grinned. "That they aren't all that bright?"

"Well, there is that." Dad chuckled. "So, back to how did they get in?"

"The two MacBooks, they could shove in their backpack, but not the desktop. That would be bulkier and pretty awkward to carry, so I'm pretty sure they either had someone along to help, which would give them another loose end, or they needed a way to cart it off."

"That's logical. What's your theory on how they got the three computers off campus? Without being seen.

Remember, the school has lights on in the dark on the school property itself, by the gym and around the football field."

"I think they would be too nervous to have someone with them. I think they rode a bike or scooter, not a four-wheeler because that would be too loud, with a basket for the HP desktop. They shoved the MacBooks in the backpack that they wore, and put the HP all-in-one monitor/CPU into the bike or scooter's basket, then rode out the way they came in — behind the baseball diamond."

Dad narrowed his eyes. "Behind the baseball diamond?"

She nodded. "There's something just beyond the trees behind the diamond. It looked like a pole. I'm thinking there's a road or house or something just beyond those trees. And if it's a road, that's an easy way for them to get home on a bike or scooter."

"Have you seen what's on the other side?" Dad asked, his interest evident in his expression.

She shook her head. "No, but I know something's there. I meant to look it up on the internet using Google Earth©, but I didn't have time."

"Let's look it up together now." Dad led the way into the living room where the family computer sat on its lonely desk.

Dad was really the only one who used the computer since Sam and her mom used their own MacBooks. He sat down and turned the computer on. Sam sat on the arm of the chair, her heart kicking up her pulse. This was the first time she and Dad had worked on an investigation together, side-by-side. She smiled. It felt pretty good.

Once he'd opened the program, he maneuvered until he had the middle school in sight. He zoomed in, until he saw the new baseball diamond and the trees behind it. Sliding his reading glasses on, he leaned closer to the monitor. "Looks like it might be Chalamont Drive backed up on the other side of those trees." He manipulated the angle until a swimming pool came into focus. "I think that's Chalamont Park."

"You know where this is?" Sam's chest tightened.

"I do." Dad turned off the computer and stood. "Let's go check it out."

Sam widened her eyes. "I can go with you?"

"Of course. It's your theory, right?"

She smiled and nodded. "Lead on."

"Let me tell your mom where we're going. You go ahead and get in the truck."

Sam raced off toward the garage, excitement thrumming through every vein. It felt brilliant to be physically following up a lead.

It felt even better to be doing it with Dad.

CHAPTER FIFTEEN

Dad turned the truck west onto Northfield Drive opposite Wal-Mart. A few miles and a roundabout later, the road turned into Chalamont Drive. At another roundabout, right across from Challain, sat the Chalamont Park with its swimming pool. Dad whipped the truck into the parking lot even though the sign read: Private: for Residents Only.

"Those look like the poles I saw," Sam said, pointing at the tall, white poles on the back of the swimming pool.

Even though it was after Labor Day, as hot as it had been in central Arkansas, the private pool was still open. Several kids jumped into the water, splashing the ladies lying poolside, soaking up summer's last rays.

Sam beat Dad out of the truck. She moved toward the little blacktop behind the parking lot, the one blocked by cement pillars. Beyond that was a double row of trees. Sam headed in that direction, Dad on her heels.

"Be careful of snakes."

That stopped her in her tracks. She could deal with a snarling dog. A hissing cat. Even a spitting ferret like her cousin Chris had, but she had the biggest fear of snakes. It didn't matter if it was a grass snake or a supposedly *good* snake that ate poisonous snakes. In Sam's opinion, the only good snake was a dead snake. Dead and chopped up into little, itty, bitty pieces.

Dad laughed and moved in front of her. "Want me to scare the *slimies* away?"

Sam smiled at the old word she'd invented for snakes when she was a child. Mom had tried to explain that snakes weren't slimy, but that they were, in fact, scaly and rough. But even as a child, Sam had shuddered and dubbed them all *slimies*. "Yeah, scare them off."

Dad took a few steps off the blacktop, then squatted.

"What are you doing?" Sam asked.

"Look." He pointed.

Closer to the bottom of the pine trees, there wasn't much foliage. From a lower position, there was a clear visual into the area past the trees.

The baseball diamond.

"We were right!" Sam moved toward the trees.

Dad grabbed her arm to stop her. "Hold up."

"A snake?" Sam froze.

"No. Evidence."

"What?"

"Your theory looks to be right. This is a direct way to the school without entering through the front gates. And it looks easy enough to ride either a scooter or a bike through."

"Then why aren't we checking it out?"

"Because there might be evidence we could destroy if we went barging in. Like tire tracks that would help us identify a certain model scooter or bike. Or a footprint if someone got off, that might help us determine the type of shoe, which could help us identify a particular brand and size. Or a myriad of other things."

She nodded.

He pointed again. "And looks like there's a little path there."

"So what do we do?"

"I call in a crime scene unit to come check it out."

Sam groaned. She hated giving up her lead. Her evidence. "How long will that take?"

Dad chuckled. "Patience is a virtue, Sam."

"Yeah, well, I missed out on it."

"It shouldn't take more than a few hours for them to make it."

"Hours? It'll be dark by then."

Dad laughed again. "Sam, it's been dark several times since the first time someone broke in. Evidence isn't scared of the dark."

"Isn't it harder to find?"

"Not with the lights we use." He grabbed his cell phone from its holder on his hip and called in the information.

"Well?" Sam asked when he hung up.

"They'll actually be out here first thing in the morning."

"The morning? But what about tonight? Isn't it supposed to rain? What if evidence like prints and stuff is washed away?" How could he wait until morning? That was crazy!

Dad shook his head. "Sam, I've got the info logged into the system. If the skies even get a big cloud, the crime scene unit will be dispatched to secure the area to protect any potential evidence."

"But what if it rains before they make it? Can't they just come now and set up, then have a cop guard it until the unit can come back out tomorrow?"

"Considering this is a mild break-in on our case roster, we can't secure the area and station security."

"Mild break-in?"

"Yes. No injuries, no damage to the property, and total stolen items valued at less than five thousand dollars. By police standards, that's a mild break-in."

It sounded logical, but Sam didn't want to accept that. It didn't seem right. "But Dad, you're giving it your attention, right?"

"Of course I am, Sam. Not just because it's your school, but because, like you, I'm pretty confident it's linked directly to the bullying issue. Sure, I'd like to get the computers back and help secure the property, but I'm more concerned with keeping everyone safe."

Dad glanced around the blacktop and the cement pillars. "And it looks like it's pretty easy to access the campus, even if the front is totally secure. That doesn't make me feel confident in the school's security to keep you kids safe."

He was right. Sam nodded. "I get it."

"Come on, I bet Mom's wondering if we found it." He led her toward the truck.

One of the older teenagers leaned against the car parked next to Dad's truck. "I haven't seen you around here. This park is for neighborhood residents only." His shoulder length hair hung in a tangle at the back of his neck. He looked out of place in this upper class subdivision. Probably still lived with his parents.

Dad pulled out his badge like a ninja boss and flashed the gold. "Little Rock Police."

The teen held up his hands in mock surrender. "Hey, no harm, no foul. Just watching out for the area like a neighborhood watch team member."

"No problem. It's smart to question people you don't recognize. Especially if kids are around." Dad pocketed his badge. "But I wonder ... an observant young man like yourself ... have you seen anyone going through that area over there?" Dad pointed toward the little path they'd found. "In the last week or so?"

The guy stared where Dad pointed, then shrugged. "Maybe. Somebody do something wrong?"

"Just asking for an investigation I'm working."

"Somebody bury a body over there or something?" The guy looked more interested than he should.

Was he serious?

"No. Nothing that gruesome that I'm aware of." Dad gave a forced little laugh. "So, have you seen anybody?"

"Maybe. A kid on a bike."

Sam grabbed Dad's arm and squeezed.

He patted her hand but remained focused on the teenager. "What'd this kid look like?"

"Man, is he in some kind of trouble or something?"

Dad shook his head. "Just want to ask him a few questions. It is a guy?"

The shaking of Dad's head, even though he never said no, must have reassured the creepy kid.

"Dunno. Can't really tell. I just assumed it was a guy, but now that you mention it, it could be a girl."

"You couldn't tell?"

"Always wears jeans and a hoodie. Keeps the hood pulled up over his head. That's why I noticed him. Or her. Who'd be wearing a hoodie when it's so blazin' hot out, ya know?"

"I'd notice that. And by a pool, too," Dad said.

"Right, man. That's what I thought."

Sam chewed her bottom lip. She'd never really gotten

to see her father question somebody on a case. He was pretty cool. The way he worked this kid — pretty epic.

"Do you recognize him or her from the neighborhood or something?"

"Can't say. With that hood over the head … but always wearing a backpack."

"Backpack?"

"Yeah. One of those heavy-duty numbers like hikers use."

"What about the bike?" Dad asked.

"A sweet Schwinn. Model is a couple of years old, but it's in good condition."

"Ah, so you're into bikes?"

The teen shrugged. "I work part-time at the Wal-Mart down the road. Sometimes I put the bikes together."

"What else can you tell me about the bike? The color? Anything unusual?"

Sam watched, respect for her father growing with every detail he pulled from the unsuspecting kid. She'd do well to learn his methods. It'd come in handy when interviewing reluctant or nervous people for stories.

"Paint was chipped, but I think it was green." He snapped his fingers. "And it had one of those quick-release mesh baskets on the front. The kind old ladies use on their bikes to get some groceries."

Sam pressed her lips together to keep her excitement from screaming out. She'd been right. About everything!

She did a victory dance inside her head while Dad got the guy's name and address, then handed him his card and told him to call him immediately if he saw the kid or bike again, or if he thought of anything else.

But Sam couldn't be still. It felt like every nerve in her body wanted to jump out of her skin. She'd been right, right, right! She wanted to jump up and down and scream but knew she couldn't. Instead, she walked back to the truck, careful not to draw any attention to herself.

She sat on the hood and stared at the people at the pool. She didn't recognize anyone, but something about the pool itself did look familiar. She didn't know why — she'd certainly never been swimming there before, but there was something about the pool ...

"I called in an update. You're getting your wish in that a team is coming out tonight."

"What changed your mind?"

Dad jabbed a thumb over his shoulder. "The kid knows I'm interested in the area and the kid on the bike. If he knows anything he wasn't willing to tell me, you can bet him or the kid will be covering tracks tonight." Dad sighed. "So the team is heading over here now."

"Can we stay and watch them work?"

"Sorry, but no. We only stay until they arrive and take charge of the site."

"But Daaadddd ..."

"Nope. Sorry. We'd only be in their way while they process the area."

She hopped off the hood and kicked a loose rock with her toe. "But we found this clue. Us. Surely we should be able to stay and at least find out if they uncover any evidence."

Dad smiled. "They'll call me as lead detective if they find anything. I can keep you posted." He smiled wider. "Off the record, of course."

She grinned back. "But of course."

● ● ●

The night lasted forever.

Despite her best attempts to sleep, Sam tossed and turned. Flipped and flopped. So much that Chewy finally got off the bed and stared up at her sadly.

10:40 p.m. She went down the hall to the bathroom. On her way back to her room, she routed herself through the living room where Mom and Dad watched the late show, cuddling together on the couch.

"Have you heard anything yet?" she asked.

Dad grinned. "They've finished setting up the lighting and closed off the area to non-official people. The unit is starting their initial purview of the path."

"Okay. Goodnight."

Mom added, "Night, my sweet girl. Maybe we can slip off tomorrow and get mani-pedis. That could be fun, yes?"

"Can Makayla come?"

"Sure."

"I'll text her. Thanks, Mom."

"Night, Pumpkin," Dad said.

Back in her room, Sam checked her email really quick. Nothing. Checked her cell phone. No messages. She sent a quick text to Mac about getting manicures and pedicures tomorrow. Makayla's mom wouldn't let her use her cell after ten, even on weekends, so Sam didn't expect to hear back until morning.

She crawled under the covers and stared at the ceiling fan. The moon shone brightly, spilling light into her room from the window. Sam pinched her eyes closed, willing herself to fall asleep.

11:21 p.m. She kicked off the covers and went to the kitchen, Chewy on her heels. After pouring a glass of milk, Sam drank it in one big gulp. She rinsed out the glass and put it in the dishwasher. Chewy whined at the door. Sam unlocked and opened the door, stepping outside with her afraid-of-the-dark dog.

Stars twinkled overhead, winking at her. Sure, they could mock her. *They* could see what was happening over at Chalamont Park.

Chewy rushed back to her from the corner. "Good girl." Sam opened the door. The dog darted in through her legs, nearly tripping her.

Sam locked the kitchen door, then headed down the hallway. Light from the television flickered from the living room.

Dad sat on the couch, Mom's sleeping head in his lap. He looked up as Sam stepped into the living room. "Just heard from the unit. They're shutting it down for the night."

Disappointment filled Sam's chest. "They didn't find anything?"

"Oh, they did." Dad grinned. "They found several sets of tire marks, all on the same back-and-forth path along the side of the baseball diamond until they disappear onto the blacktop behind the school."

Nothing in her body could sleep now. "So we were totally right?"

He smiled and nodded. "Looks like it."

"We rock!"

Dad chuckled. Mom stirred.

"I'd better get her to bed." Dad gently rubbed Mom's shoulder.

"What's next?" Sam asked as Mom sat up and wiped her eyes.

"In the morning, they'll take casts of the tire tracks and get to talking to a bike expert who might be able to match these tires to a Schwinn like our friend in the park mentioned."

"What do we do?" She wanted to run out and do something right now.

He shook his head and helped Mom to her feet. "We do nothing. I'll get a team to do a neighborhood canvas to try and find the bike. If we can find the owner, we might be able to bring them in for questioning."

"That's it?" She just expected there to be ... well, more to a police investigation when a big clue had been uncovered.

Mom leaned over and planted a kiss on Sam's forehead. "Goodnight, my sweet girl." She shuffled sleepily to her bedroom.

"Night, Mom."

Dad gave her arm a squeeze. "We'll also put out the word about the three stolen computers to local pawn shops. Maybe one of them has the computers, so we can go question them and review their surveillance video. Sometimes those leads are what break a case wide open."

Still, Sam thought there would be more.

Dad kissed her cheek. "Get some rest. There's nothing else to do or learn tonight."

Waiting wasn't something she embraced. It went too much hand-in-hand with patience. Virtue or not, Sam didn't like waiting.

And being patient was highly overrated.

CHAPTER SIXTEEN

Nail salons had a distinctively gross smell, Sam thought. All of them stank the same. A stench that couldn't be masked by nail polish or nail polish remover.

Sam sat in a whirlpool chair between her mother and Makayla.

Mom laid her head against the massage chair and closed her eyes. "Ahh. This is heavenly."

Sam grinned at her best friend. "Dad was going into the office today to see whatever the team turned up." She'd brought Makayla up to speed on the drive to the nail salon in Chenal Promenade.

"That is so cool."

"Yeah. We hope to get a lead on whoever is behind bullying Nikki and stealing the EAST lab's computers."

"You seem pretty certain it's the same person."

Sam nodded. "It would help if I could find out each

of their whereabouts on Tuesday evening, when the email was sent to Nikki."

Mom sat up. "Who are your suspects?" Clearly, she'd been eavesdropping, but Sam took no offense. It was a journalism staple.

"Well, first there's Felicia Adams. She transferred to our school last month after she got expelled from her private school. She's bitter about being forced to attend a public school and not being allowed to participate in any extra-curricular activities." Sam pressed the button to restart the massage chair's cycle. "Felicia has a crush on Thomas Murphy, who has a crush on Nikki Cole. And Nikki asked him to escort her at the homecoming pep rally."

"She has a history of discipline problems. She's a regular in Mrs. Creegle's office," Makayla added. Even Mac felt comfortable enough speaking freely in front of Mom, understanding that her questions were from a reporter's point of view.

"Okay. Who's next?" Mom asked.

"Billy Costiff. He's a nerdy-type eighth grader who has a crush on Nikki." Sam paused, considering the circumstances. "Well, more than a crush, the guy was obsessed with her. Followed her all over campus, pushed letters through her locker slots ... all kinds of creepy stuff that made her feel uncomfortable." Sam twitched as the pedicurist ran a brush over the bottom of her foot, then giggled. She was so ticklish on her feet.

"But a few weeks ago, Nikki talked to Mrs. Trees and Mrs. Creegle about him," Makayla continued.

"Nikki said he now glares at her and really unnerves her. Like instead of being good obsessed, he's stalker-like."

Mom chuckled. "There's a good obsessed?"

Sam grinned. "You know what I mean, Mom."

"I do. Who else?"

"Melanie Olson," Makayla volunteered.

Sam nodded. "Her father was one of the Hewlett Packard plant workers laid off by Nikki's mother. Because her father lost his job, Melanie's family had to downsize. They now live in an apartment instead of the big house they were in, and she's late to school a lot because they haven't changed the bus route yet." She rested her head against the chair, letting the kneading option on the massage work between her shoulder blades. "And she's really mad that Mrs. Cole still has her job and is able to keep living in her pretty house with Nikki and Jefferson."

"Yeah, she's gone out of her way to avoid even looking at Nikki," Makayla said.

"I see. Who else?" Mom asked.

"Well," Sam sat upright in the chair, her voice vibrating as the chair pounded on her lower back. "I think Aubrey Damas could be involved."

"I thought you said she was Nikki's best friend." Mom handed the manicurist the nail polish she'd picked out.

"She is," Makayla answered.

"But she doesn't act like it. She's so jealous that Nikki got nominated for homecoming court and she didn't. Nikki says Aubrey hasn't really talked to her since the announcement." Sam sat still while the pedicurist drained the water from the whirlpool and dried her feet.

"But the letter and text were already sent to Nikki before the announcement was made," Makayla said.

"I know. That has me stumped because I was watching Nikki and Aubrey when the announcement was made and Aubrey was totally surprised." Sam shook her head and handed her polish to the pedicurist. "No way is Aubrey a good enough actress to fake the shock I saw on her face."

"Then she really isn't a suspect," Mom said.

"Well," Sam shrugged, "she could be working with someone. I mean, Nikki's positive no one besides her and Aubrey have the combination to her locker. If that's true, how'd the diet bars get in there?"

"A good point to consider," Mom said. "Anybody else?"

"That's all I've got." Sam let out a low breath as the manicurist started on her nails while the pedicurist painted her toes.

"So you need to find out where they were during the time the email was sent to Nikki?"

"Yes, ma'am," Makayla answered. "Tuesday evening at 6:44."

"I'm assuming neither of you are close enough friends with any of them to just ask?" Mom asked.

"Not hardly." Sam had a mental image of her hanging out with Aubrey.

Makayla shuddered. "Definitely not."

"Do you know anybody who is close friends with any of them?"

Sam had to think about that one. "I don't think anyone's close with Felicia. She gives off a snobbish vibe, and she's new."

"I know Melanie Olson okay. Her mom and my mom are in a prayer group together. I could try to find out where she was on Tuesday night," Makayla said.

"Thanks, Mac." Sam chewed her bottom lip. "I don't know Billy well, and I don't know anyone who really does." She remembered the EAST roster from Mrs. Trees' computer. "He and Aubrey both have EAST in first period, though."

"That doesn't prove they're working together to bully Nikki," Makayla said.

"No, it doesn't," Sam said. "But it proves they do know each other. They share at least one class together."

"How do you know Aubrey and Billy's schedule, Sam?" Mom asked.

Sam's face burned, and she swallowed. "I don't. I just know they both have EAST for first period."

"I see." Mom's expression said she understood more than Sam would tell her.

Good thing Mom understood sources and confidential information. A whole lot more than Dad. Otherwise, she'd be in some hot water.

Boiling hot.

● ● ●

Maggie Moo's was nice and cold. Perfect when it was so hot, humid, and miserable outside. Where was fall? Wasn't the end of September supposed to bring cooler temperatures? The crazy Arkansas weather was fooling them all again.

"Thank you, Mrs. Sanderson," Makayla said as the three of them sat at one of the tables.

"My pleasure. I'll be honest — I love getting my nails done and having an ice cream. Inviting you two girls gives me an excuse to give in to my guilty pleasure."

Sam grinned and shoved a spoon of chocolate fudge ice cream in her mouth. She closed her eyes and savored the creamy goodness as it melted on her tongue. Ice cream just made her happy, plain and simple. People said you couldn't buy happiness, but Sam suspected if more people bought ice cream, the world would be a happier place.

"I don't believe it," Makayla said.

Sam opened her eyes to stare at her friend.

"Look." Makayla jerked her head toward the front door.

Trying to look casual, Sam turned in her seat to see what had gotten Makayla's attention.

Billy Costiff and Marcus Robertson opened the door and stepped inside.

"That's Billy Costiff," Sam leaned over and whispered to her mother.

"Oh." Mom stood. "Sam, I need to run into the Nike store to grab Dad a shirt they had on sale. I'll be back in a few minutes. Enjoy your ice cream." She winked at Sam, then left.

Mom was so utterly cool!

"Hey, Sam," Marcus said as soon as Mom had left.

"Hi, Marcus." She smiled at Billy. "Hi, Billy."

"You know Sam Sanderson, right?" Marcus asked Billy.

"Yeah." Billy nodded at her. "Hey."

"This is Makayla Ansley," Sam introduced them.

Both guys stood there, awkwardly holding their cones.

"Why don't y'all sit with us?" Sam asked.

"Sure." Marcus looked at Billy. "Okay?"

They all sat and an uneasy silence settled over them. Sam took another bite of her ice cream then looked at Marcus. "Hey, I heard you'll be escorting Frannie to the pep rally. Does that mean you'll be in a suit?"

"Yeah, I guess." He turned red. "I'm taking her to the dance, too."

"That's really cool," Makayla said.

Marcus smiled at her over the table. "Thanks. We're just friends."

Uh-oh. Sam could see the sparks here. Frannie would *not* be happy. Better get to the point. "So, Billy ... are you going to the homecoming dance, too?" Sam asked.

Makayla shot her an ugly look. The one that said, "Could you be any more blunt and obvious?"

Sam ignored her.

"Uh, yeah."

Marcus looked at his friend. "You are?"

"I asked Kathy Gibbs." Billy smiled shyly. "She said yes. Finally."

Sam nearly choked on her ice cream. Kathy Gibbs? She was an eighth grader staff reporter for the newspaper. Kinda kept to herself but nice. She didn't really talk a lot with the other kids. "I have newspaper with her. She's nice."

Billy nodded. "She is. We go to church together, and I've wanted to ask her out since last year but got a little sidetracked by another girl." He glanced out the window and stared absently toward the movie theater. "Things got a little weird, and I wanted to explain and apologize, but that just didn't happen. Anyway, it's all over now."

Marcus gave his friend a mock punch. "That's cool. Sam and I both have newspaper with Kathy. I can't believe she hasn't said anything. There's been so much talk about homecoming in the paper ... who's escorting who, who will be named homecoming queen … all that girl stuff."

"Hey! I'm not talking about it all the time," Sam said.

"Not you," Marcus smiled.

"Well, I just asked her Tuesday night."

If Sam were a dog, her ears would've perked up. "Tuesday night?"

Billy nodded. "Yeah. She's in my youth group at church, and we had a pizza party Tuesday night. I asked her then." His cheeks turned red again. "I was a little surprised she said yes, but I'm glad she did."

Sam could see that. "You two make a cute couple."

He chuckled. "Really? Thanks."

"What about you two? Are y'all going to the dance?" Marcus asked.

Makayla shook her head. "Not me. My mom won't let me go to a dance until I'm in high school."

"Even a school one?" Marcus asked.

"She won't even let me go to ones at church." Makayla sighed loudly. "My mom's a little over-protective these days."

"That's putting it mildly," Sam said. "Her mom only lets her go out as much as she does because my dad asks."

Makayla nodded. "It's true. Because Sam's dad is a cop, Mom thinks if he says Sam's going, then it's safe."

"As if I have a team of security guards following me around or something." Sam chuckled.

"But we haven't been able to get Mom to relent on dances."

"That bites," Marcus said.

"Tell me about it." Makayla sighed for effect.

"What about you?" Marcus asked Sam. "You going to the dance?"

"I don't know yet." Maybe she should feel embarrassed that no one had asked her, but she didn't. "Maybe."

At the moment, she cared more about the fact that Billy Costiff had an alibi for the time the email to Nikki was sent. He was no longer a suspect.

That only left Felicia, Melanie, and possibly Aubrey.

Sam wondered if the crime scene unit had better luck with the tire casts, or if the investigating officers got a lead from their questioning of the neighborhood residents, or if they had any luck finding the computers at the pawn shops.

She finished off her ice cream, ready for Mom to come back so they could leave. Sam couldn't wait to call Dad and find out how the investigation went. She wanted to be a part of it, even if she couldn't report on it. At least she could share the information with Nikki to put in her article.

Especially if Aubrey was involved. That would be too *sa-weet*!

CHAPTER SEVENTEEN

Were all churches soothing? There was just something so peaceful about walking into the sanctuary of her church, Sam felt. Maybe it was because she'd attended West Little Rock all her life. Maybe it was the rocking worship band. Sam didn't know, but she always felt better about everything when she was there.

"See you before the service," Mom said as she and Dad turned to head to the adult Sunday school classrooms.

Sam nodded and made her way to the youth room. It had occurred to Sam late last night that since Billy had an alibi, that meant the bully and thief had to be a girl. She'd done a lot of research on girl bullies into the early hours of the morning. Female bullying was a sub-type of bullying. Who knew? It was crazy.

Some studies made it clear that female bullying was just as prominent and severe as bullying from guys. Female bullying could sometimes even be worse. Females were most typically associated with cyber bullying, indirect bullying, and the social alienation type of bullying.

Sounded just like Nikki's bully. If Sam would've done more research sooner, she might not have wasted time and energy thinking Billy Costiff was a suspect.

Either way, she couldn't wait to tell Makayla. She hurried down the hall, then turned into the youth room. She waved at Lissi as she entered, heading straight to the overstuffed loveseat where she and Makayla always sat. She came to an abrupt halt.

"Hey, Sam. Look who's going to start coming to our church." Makayla sat beside none other than Melanie Olson.

"Hi, Melanie." Sam was quick to smile. Even though Melanie was a suspect, Sam really felt sorry for her. It had to be awful for your dad to lose his job and for your family to suffer through so many changes.

"Hi." Melanie didn't look very happy. Matter of fact, she looked downright miserable.

Sam dropped onto the loveseat next to Makayla. It was a snug fit, but she didn't care, and she knew Mac didn't mind being squished. "I guess Makayla intro-duced you around?"

Melanie nodded.

"This is a great group. We've gotten pretty close."

"I loved my group," Melanie said.

Sam licked her lips. "What happened?"

She shrugged. "It's in Conway, where my dad used to work. We're having to cut all costs, even gas money, so Mom said we needed to find a church closer to where we live."

"You drove to Conway every Sunday?" Sam asked.

Melanie frowned at her. "Yeah. It's only like thirty or so minutes. My dad used to drive it every day to and from work. It's not a big deal."

"Oh." Sam didn't know what to say.

Luckily, Ms. Martha called the group to order with a prayer, then greeted everyone. Makayla introduced Melanie. "This is my friend, Melanie Olson. She attends my school and has been going to church in Conway, but her mother would like them to find a church a little closer to home, so they're visiting us."

Ms. Martha smiled. "Welcome, Melanie. We're happy to have you here. I'm sure you'll fit right in."

"I fit in at my church just fine," Melanie mumbled under her breath. Only Makayla and Sam could hear since they were on the loveseat beside her.

Ms. Martha had already moved her attention to the Scripture for today. "There have been a lot of changes in our community lately. In our church families. In the state." She smiled. "Our whole nation, really. It can be scary sometimes, and sad, but also exciting. This past week, I had some surprising news that will change mine and my husband's life. It was a little scary, but very exciting, and it got me to thinking about all the different times in my life."

Everyone was silent, hanging onto Ms. Martha's every word.

"I thought about how when I was a child, all I knew was my own little circle. That was my world. My parents, my brother, my home, and my church." She smiled. "My world was pretty small, and it kinda revolved all around me."

Everybody laughed. Hard to picture Ms. Martha being self-centered. She was one of the most giving people Sam had ever met.

"Then I started school, and my world grew. I had friends and teachers and youth, but the focus was still really all about me." Ms. Martha paused. "But as I grew older, my awareness of the world outside of me seeped into my reality. At first it was on a community and state level. Tornado destruction, missing children in the area, heroic firemen … stuff like that." Her smile had subsided. "Then awareness of the world came into my life. World hunger, wars, terrorists, people banding together after tragedies to help one another."

Silence settled over the youth room as everyone

remembered the changes in their lives. Sam couldn't help but think about the big change she'd be facing in her life if Mom took the *National Geographic* offer. That would be a big personal change, but nothing like the changes Mom would see of the world.

"The Scripture I selected for today is Ecclesiastes 3:1–8. I think most of you will recognize it. Sandy, would you please read it aloud for us?"

Sandy flipped through her Bible. "There is a time for everything, and a season for every activity under the heavens: a time to be born and a time to die, a time to plant and a time to uproot, a time to kill and a time to heal, a time to tear down and a time to build, a time to weep and a time to laugh, a time to mourn and a time to dance, a time to scatter stones and a time to gather them, a time to embrace and a time to refrain from embracing, a time to search and a time to give up, a time to keep and a time to throw away, a time to tear and a time to mend, a time to be silent and a time to speak, a time to love and a time to hate, a time for war and a time for peace."

"The Bible tells us that we will always have changes in our lives. What do y'all think it means to you?" Ms. Martha asked.

"I think it's God telling us that we'll go through good times and bad, but it's okay, because there's a time for everything," Daniel said.

"To me, it means that even when I'm going through a

really hard time, it won't last, because a time for something else will come along soon," Ava Kate offered.

"Good." Ms. Martha smiled. "Anybody else?"

"It's almost a push-pull type of thing to me," Sam said.

"How's that?" Ms. Martha asked.

Sam stared at the Scripture in the Bible app on her iPad. "Well, look at each verse ... a mention of almost opposites: be born and die, plant and uproot, kill and heal, tear down and build, cry and laugh, mourn and dance, love and hate ... every verse."

"It does, so what does that mean to you?" Ms. Martha asked.

Sam shrugged. "I'm not entirely sure, but everything we deal with, we'll have to go from one extreme to the other to grow. Even when I'm mad and give everyone the silent treatment, it's okay, because there's the time for that. But I can't stay mad and silent forever. That time will end, and I'll have to reach the opposite end where I'm talking and sharing my feelings."

"Very good." Ms. Martha winked at Sam. "Anybody else?"

"It's reassuring to me," Sandy said, "in that it feels like this Scripture gives me permission to let myself have the emotions that we, as Christians, sometimes forget it's okay to feel. Like hatred, giving up, killing." She shook her head. "Not in the literal sense. Y'all know what I mean."

"Yeah, stay away from Sandy. She's deadly," Jeremy joked.

"I know what you mean, Sandy." Ms. Martha said. "Christians should strive to emulate Christ, so we should love and forgive, but let's not forget that Jesus had righteous anger. Remember he flipped the money-changers' table over."

Everyone chuckled.

"Anybody else?" Ms. Martha asked.

"Yeah," Sam said. "Since you brought it up, what change are you and your husband about to face?"

Ms. Martha smiled. "I should have known the reporter in the group wouldn't let it slide." Her smile widened and her hands automatically went to her tummy. "About the time y'all get out of school in May, I'll be ready to have our baby!"

Everyone chimed in with shouts and claps of congratulations. The girls got up to give her hugs, but Sam noticed Melanie still sitting alone on the loveseat, staring at the open Bible in her lap. It occurred to Sam that she'd just assumed the lesson today was God's sign to her to accept it if Mom took the assignment. Maybe she'd been wrong.

Maybe the lesson today had been for Melanie, to accept the changes she had no control over, like her dad losing his job.

"Let's close in prayer so we aren't late to Pastor

Patterson's service," Ms. Martha said after getting her final hug from Lissi.

After prayer, most everyone headed toward the sanctuary. Sam and Makayla hung back a little to walk with Melanie.

"What did you think about the group?" Makayla asked.

Melanie shrugged. "It was okay. Kinda nice." She glanced at Makayla. "Did you ask her to talk about change because I was here?"

"Of course not. Ms. Martha picks out lessons she thinks are important. You heard her: she's gonna have a baby, which is a big change." Makayla's defenses showed.

Sam smiled and nudged Melanie. "Yeah, don't make it all about you." She kept her voice light and her smile in place to show she was teasing.

Melanie smiled back. "Yeah, you're right."

"Hey, Melanie and her family are coming to our house for lunch after church. You wanna come?" Makayla asked.

Sam shook her head. "Can't. I promised Nikki I'd drop by and help her with the article for the school blog. She has to set it to post early, so she just wanted me to look it over for her."

"That's nice," Mac said.

"You know, you were right about her mom not

having a choice in laying off all those people," Melanie offered. She let out a sigh.

Mac gave Melanie a sideways hug as they stopped outside the church's main doors. "It's a hard situation."

Melanie smiled. "No, a hard situation was every night this past week. We had to sort through all the boxes we'd just put in storage, deciding what we would keep and what we had to get rid of because we needed to move our stuff to a smaller storage unit. I think we got to bed at ten every night this week."

"Well then, you'll really enjoy lunch. Mom made her homemade, three-layer chocolate cake. It's amazing, right, Sam?" Makayla said as she led the way into the sanctuary.

"It's out of this world," Sam agreed, but her mind stuttered over Melanie's words.

She'd just lost another suspect.

"Try writing it something like this," Sam took over Nikki's keyboard and typed.

Nikki nodded. "Oh, that's good." She grinned. "Thanks."

Heat whooshed up the back of Sam's neck. "No problem."

"No, you're really, really good at this. You're going to

make a great reporter. I mean, you already are, but you know what I mean."

"I hope so." Man, did she ever hope so. "Anyway, I think it's ready for you to set to post now."

"I appreciate you coming over and helping me today." Nikki opened the notebook sitting by her desk. "I can't remember the passcode to the paper's blog. I can't remember anything." She grinned and waved her spiral notebook. "I have to write down every password and code and login I use in this thing. If I lose it, I'm locked out of my whole life."

"I'm lucky that I can remember things pretty easy," Sam replied.

"You're lucky all right." Nikki set the article to upload to the school's newspaper's blog at five-thirty in the morning. "This is the first big assignment Aubrey gave me. She usually assigns me the fashion articles. Not that I mind that, of course. Fashion's more my scene anyway."

"Yeah." Sam could only think of one reason Aubrey would assign this to Nikki — to make her uncomfortable and upset her.

That said a lot about Aubrey's personality right there.

"Anyway," Nikki sighed.

"I don't want to bring up a sore subject, but have you gotten any more letters or texts or packages?"

Nikki shook her head. "No, thank goodness. I'm

thinking maybe the person's done, like Dad said from the beginning — gave up or moved on."

"I don't think that's it. I think they've just got other things occupying them at the moment. Like breaking into the school to steal the computer they sent the email from to cover her tracks, and — "

"*Her* tracks?"

Sam shrugged. "Most of my suspects are females. Did you know that female bullying is actually a recognized form of bullying? Isn't that crazy?" Maybe Nikki wouldn't push it. Maybe she wouldn't ask. It would be really bad to have to tell Nikki that Sam suspected Aubrey, her best friend, of being involved in such a hurtful campaign against Nikki.

Nikki shook her head. "I'm tired of hearing about all the bullying, to be honest, Sam."

Because she wanted to pretend like she wasn't a victim. "I understand, Nikki, I do, but you do realize the bully started with you for a reason. Something we haven't figured out is why you were picked to be the victim. I doubt it'll all just go away without having figured that out."

Nikki stood and shut her laptop. "Well, thanks again for coming by. I've got to start getting ready for dinner. Dad's coming by and taking us all out to eat."

That was her cue that the conversation was over, and it was time to go. "Oh." Sam stood. "Not to be nosy, but does this mean your mom and dad aren't getting a divorce?"

"I don't really know. I mean, they were at each other's throats and fighting all the time until Dad moved out. Even then, they would still yell at each other on the phone and would hardly speak when they saw each other."

Sam wanted to cringe. Even with Mom's offer and Mom and Dad not agreeing, they weren't yelling at each other all the time. Sam didn't know if she could take that.

Nikki paused at her bedroom door. "Then Jefferson got hurt, and they put aside everything to make sure he was okay. Then all this stuff with me started, so Dad's been spending more time around here. He and Mom aren't fighting anymore. I haven't heard them talk about meeting with the lawyer in weeks, so, who knows?"

Sam gave Nikki's arm a squeeze. "I'm praying it all works out."

"Thanks." Nikki smiled and opened her bedroom door. "Now I have to hurry to the shower so I can get in there before Jefferson. He uses all the hot water." She led the way to the front of the house.

"That's one of the great things about being an only child." Sam fell into step alongside Nikki. "Where is Jefferson? I didn't see him when I came in."

"He's at some friend's pool party, again. Today's the last day for the community pool to be open, so the Chalamont neighborhood had a cook-out and pool party to celebrate." Nikki opened the front door. "Thanks again, Sam. You've really been a good friend and everything."

Certainly better than Aubrey. Sam smiled. "Any time. If you need anything, just call."

"I will."

"Have fun tonight. Bye." Sam turned and strode to the sidewalk, heading toward home.

Such an interesting turn of events with Nikki's mom and dad. Like the verses today at church ... there was a time for everything. Maybe a time for Nikki's parents to separate, and a time for them to come back together.

Sam smiled as she thought about it. Funny how a hurt ankle could help heal a marriage.

CHAPTER EIGHTEEN

I found a letter in my locker."

Sam turned away from the layout she'd been looking at with Lana to stare at Nikki. "What?"

Nikki motioned her to follow her.

"I'll be back in a second," Sam told Lana as she stood and followed Nikki to an empty table in the newspaper room.

Nikki pulled a folded piece of paper out of her pocket and handed it to Sam. "I found this in my locker just before I came here."

Sam unfolded it and read:

YOU ARE FAT AND UGLY AND SHOULD BE HIDDEN FROM THE WORLD

This went beyond cruel. Sam's hand shook as she

held the horrid letter. "Nikki, whoever this is, they aren't going to just stop. Your dad is wrong. You need to take this to the police, and tell them everything. If you want, you can just talk to my dad and his partner."

Nikki shook her head, but she couldn't shake the tears. "I don't understand why someone hates me so much."

"I told you, it's about power, but I think you were picked specifically as the victim. We just need to figure out — "

"What's this?" Aubrey grabbed the letter from Sam's hands. Her eyes widened as she read. "Samantha Sanderson, have you been sending these letters to poor Nikki?" Her voice carried across the newspaper's classroom.

"Shh." Nikki snatched the letter back. "Don't be stupid, Aub. You know Sam wouldn't do something like this."

"Do I?" Aubrey didn't lower her voice as she smirked at Sam.

Ms. Pape stood behind her desk. "Girls, is there a problem?"

"No, ma'am," Nikki answered, glaring at Aubrey. "What's your problem?" she asked in a whisper.

"I don't know, Nikki. Think about it. Sam sure seems to be at the right place at the right time for you to share such information with her. And she was supposed to get suspended for not *giving up her sources*, but she was right back in class the very next day, right?" Aubrey shook her head and crossed her arms over her chest. "Seems kinda fishy to me. And wasn't she out by your locker when you found the diet bars?"

Nikki stared at Sam.

"Aw, come on, Nikki. You know better. I've been the one trying to help you." Sam turned to Aubrey. "What about you?"

"Me?" Aubrey's voice went shrill.

"You're so jealous and spiteful about Nikki being nominated to homecoming court instead of you that you can't even be excited for her. She's supposed to be your best friend." Sam's voice, like Aubrey's, carried across the room.

Ms. Pape rushed over as everyone else fell silent. "Girls!" She moved them toward the corner. "What's going on?"

Aubrey grabbed the letter back from Nikki and handed it to Ms. Pape. "Nikki's been getting letters like this. Texts. And someone put diet bars in her locker."

Ms. Pape put an arm around Nikki's shoulders. "Nikki, why haven't you said anything? This is bullying." Her mouth formed a perfect "O" as she nodded at Sam. "That's why you suggested a series on bullying."

Sam nodded.

"And don't you find that mighty convenient?" Aubrey nudged Nikki. "She was just coming off as a lead reporter on the movie theater story and was taking a backseat on assignments. She sure needed something to write about to put her back at the top of the newspaper's blog."

"That's crazy. Bullying is a huge issue. I've been working to stop bullying, in case you haven't noticed." Sam's hands really shook now. She balled them into tight fists.

"Maybe you just want people to think that. Acting all better than everyone else. Maybe it's just an act so no one will suspect you."

"Oh, puhleeze, Aubrey. You're really crazier than I thought." Sam shook her head. "You know Nikki's locker combination. Only you and she know it, so it seems to point the suspicious finger to you about how those diet bars got in the locker." Sam popped her fists on her hips. "Explain that."

"I don't have to explain anything to you, *Samantha Sanderson*."

"No, but you'd better get your explanation lined up before the police question you." Sam pressed her lips together so tight it hurt. Man, she really, really, *really* wanted to give Aubrey Damas a piece of her mind.

"Are you gonna call your daddy on me now?" Aubrey used her fake sing-song tone.

"We'll take this to Mrs. Trees' office," Ms. Pape said.

"No!" Nikki's face went pale. "I don't want anyone to know about this."

"It's a little late for that," Sam said, gesturing toward the class.

Big tears filled Nikki's eyes.

The anger shot out of Sam. "I'm sorry, Nikki," she whispered.

"You should be sorry," Aubrey said.

Sam snapped. "Just shut up, Aubrey. No one wants to hear your ugliness."

Aubrey's eyes grew as large as half dollars, her jaw dropped, leaving her mouth hanging open, and her face turned pink. Then red.

No one made a sound.

Her face turned redder.

Ms. Pape even remained silent, just staring at Aubrey's ever-reddening face.

Sam swallowed and kept staring at Aubrey. Backing down was so not an option.

Aubrey closed her mouth tight enough that a white ring formed around the edge of her lips. "I can't believe you have the nerve to — "

"Nerve? Are you serious? Aubrey, you want to be a queen so badly? No worries. You are crowned the biggest drama queen at Robinson Middle School."

"That's enough, girls. Let's go." Ms. Pape folded the letter. "Class, I'll be back in a few minutes. I trust you'll behave."

"Please, Ms. Pape ..." Nikki began.

"I'm sorry, Nikki. Teachers are required to report any form of bullying they have knowledge of. I can't *not* report this."

The tears slipped down Nikki's cheeks as Ms. Pape, arm still around Nikki's shoulders, led the way to the office.

"See what you've done," Aubrey hissed at Sam as they followed.

Sam's temper heated again. "Me? You're the one who intruded on a private conversation. You're the one who took the letter and read it, even though Nikki hadn't given you permission. You're the one who yelled out Nikki's personal business so everyone in the room could hear." Sam shook her head. "Yeah, Aubrey, as usual, blame everything on any and everybody but yourself. It must be so tiring to be such a major pain in the behind all the time."

"You're so crude, Samantha."

"And you're so jealous."

"Of you? Not hardly," Aubrey stuck her nose higher in the air.

"You're jealous of anyone who gets any attention. What's the matter, Aubrey? Mommy and Daddy don't dote on you enough at home?"

"You shut up, Samantha Sanderson."

"Girls!" Ms. Pape turned to glare at them before she opened the office door.

Felicia Adams sat on the bench outside Mrs. Trees' office. Ms. Pape pointed to the bench. "You two sit here and wait until Mrs. Trees is ready to deal with you. Come along, Nikki."

Aubrey sat on the far end of the bench, as far away as humanly possible from Felicia. No way was Sam going to sit between them. She'd had about all of Aubrey that she could stand. She chose to stand on the other side of Felicia.

"Hey, do-gooder, what're you doing in here again?" Felicia smiled at Sam. "You trying to roughen up your reputation?"

"Nope, just having to deal with Ms. Drama down there." Sam jerked her head in Aubrey's direction.

"You wish," Aubrey said.

Felicia twisted to face Aubrey. "What? Did you say something, princess?"

Aubrey turned her head to stare out the door opposite Felicia and Sam.

Felicia chuckled and looked back at Sam. "I don't think the princess likes me very much."

"She doesn't like anybody very much, except herself."

"Nicely done, do-gooder." Felicia smiled, her eyebrows raised.

It was getting harder and harder to think of Felicia as a bad person when Sam was really beginning to like her. Now that she was getting to know more about Felicia, Sam couldn't really see her taking the time to send letters or texts or break into the school to send emails to Nikki. She seemed so much more the in-your-face type.

If Felicia wasn't a suspect, that only left Aubrey. Even

though Sam detested her and thought she might be involved, she didn't think Aubrey was the sole bully.

That meant there was someone else. Another guilty party, and Sam had no clue who it could be.

"I can't believe Aubrey did that." Makayla threw herself across Sam's bed and reached over to rub Chewy's belly. Her parents had a cooking class they attended once a month, so Makayla came home with Sam those afternoons. Both girls loved it.

"She totally humiliated Nikki in front of the whole newspaper staff." Sam paced. "Nikki bawled when Mrs. Trees called her parents."

"They already knew, right?"

Sam nodded. "But they'd been telling her to toughen up and ride it out until the bully moved on to someone else. Nikki didn't want them to see this last letter. It went beyond brutally cruel."

"Maybe now her parents will realize how serious this is and call the police."

"Her parents don't have a choice. Neither does Nikki." Sam plopped down on the foot of the bed. "Once an incident of bullying is reported to the school and documented, law enforcement must be called in."

"But you didn't see any police this afternoon?"

Sam shook her head. "Mrs. Trees lectured me

and Aubrey about fighting, but then had to let us go because it was close to dismissal time. Nikki had to stay in the office until her parents came to talk with Mrs. Trees."

"I feel so sorry for Nikki," Makayla said.

"Me, too." Sam toed her backpack. "Do you have any homework you need to work on? I don't want your mom to get all mad about you not doing it and not let you come over on a school night again."

"Nope, did it all in study hall."

Sam grinned and gave her a nudge. "Look at you, being all smart and stuff."

"I'm a ninja like that, remember?" Makayla laughed. "Do you have any?"

"Nope. Finished mine in class." Sam stretched and lay back on the bed. "What do you want to do? Mom's got dinner all handled so she doesn't need any help."

"Why don't you have a swimming pool?" Makayla moved to the window in Sam's bedroom. "There's a perfect spot for it right back there." She tapped her finger against the window.

"I wish. It's still so hot and sticky outside."

"If you had a pool, we could swim even when every other pool had already closed for the winter." Makayla pressed her forehead against the window. "It doesn't feel like anything should be closing for winter."

Sam smiled. "Yeah. I always hated that pools — " She bolted upright. "Wait a minute." Her mind whirred.

"What?" Makayla moved from the window and sat in Sam's desk chair.

"Hang on." Sam raised a finger. Something was there, just on the edge of her thoughts. Pool. Closing. Cookout. Party.

She snapped her fingers. "Jefferson."

Makayla shrugged. "What about him?"

Sam's chest tightened. This was *it*! She could feel it. "Jefferson was at a party yesterday to celebrate the last day before the neighborhood pool closed. Chalamont Park's pool." The thoughts were spinning around in her head so fast she could barely make out the blur.

"Oh-kay. What am I missing?"

"Chalamont Park's pool is near the road behind the baseball diamond."

Makayla shook her head. "Still not following you, Sam."

"When we were at the baseball diamond, did you know what was behind it?"

"Uh, no. And I didn't want to stick around to find out. It was a good thing Officer Bill is such a nice guy, or we could've gotten in big trouble."

Sam crossed her legs and all but bounced on her bed. "Forget all that. We didn't know what was back there because we'd never been on the other side, right?"

"I guess." Makayla still wore the dazed and confused look.

"So whoever broke into the school, both times, needed to know what was behind the baseball diamond and where it went ..."

Makayla smiled. "Which means it had to be somebody who'd been at the pool and knew about the path to the baseball diamond."

"Right. Jefferson."

"Wait. What? You lost me again."

"Jefferson is familiar enough with the area. Nikki said he was there *again*, meaning he'd been there before. By the way she said it, kind of sounded like he'd been there quite a bit."

"You think *Jefferson* might be the bully? Nikki's his sister."

Sam nodded. "He told me he didn't know the letters and texts were illegal. That line of thinking would make sense if it was a brother sending them to his sister."

"But why? He saw how upset it made her. Why would he keep on? I don't know him well, but he doesn't strike me as just being cruel and hateful. Sibling rivalry is one thing, but this is so much more than that."

"I would think that, too, but then I realized I'd already given myself the answer."

"Please," Makayla said as she leaned back in the chair. "Enlighten me."

"To get his parents back together. Nikki said that because of the letters and texts, her dad had been coming over more often and not fighting with her mom when he did. The first note might have been out of sibling rivalry or a fight between them, but if Jefferson noticed the change in his parents after that, which I'm pretty sure he did, then he would have to keep on hurting Nikki to keep his dad coming over."

Makayla tapped her finger against her chin. "Maybe. But you have no proof."

"No, but when you think of Jefferson as the bully, everything makes sense."

"I can see that, but, again, how do you prove it?"

Sam jumped up off the bed, scaring Chewy into Mac's lap. "The bike. If he has one of those green Schwinn's like the kid at the park described to Dad, then there's the proof."

"Not exactly enough to be 100% positive."

"Enough to take to Dad." She grabbed her cell and dialed Nikki's phone. "Please pick up, please pick up, please pick up."

"Hey, Sam. I'm a little busy right now. Can I call you back?" Nikki's voice sounded hoarse like Sam's did after cheering all night.

Sam put the call on speaker. "I just have a quick question: does Jefferson have a bike?"

"Yeah. He's on it all the time. Why?"

"What kind and color? Do you know?"

"Uh, yeah. It's a Schwinn, just like mine. We got them for Christmas a couple of years ago. His is green and mine is red."

"Thanks. I know you're busy, so I'll let you go. Call me later." She hung up the phone and danced around the room.

"That doesn't necessarily mean Jefferson's the one." But Makayla set Chewy on the floor and danced along with Sam.

"Now it all makes sense. I can't wait until Dad gets home."

She had figured it all out!

CHAPTER NINETEEN

Headlight beams shot through the front window. Chewy ran to the garage door, barking like crazy.

"Finally!" Sam rushed to the door almost as excited to see Dad as Chewy. Mom followed at a much more sedate pace.

Dad had stayed late at work, working on the bullying case, Sam's mom had told her. It was nearly nine now, and Makayla's parents had picked her up over an hour ago, leaving Sam alone to wait. And wait. And wait.

Patience so wasn't Sam's strong point.

The door opened, and Dad stepped inside. "Well, hello. Isn't this a sight, my girls here to greet me at the door?" He gave Mom a kiss, then, as usual, he went immediately to his and Mom's room to lock up his gun and badge.

Sam followed. "Dad, I need to talk to you."

He finished locking the gun and set his shield beside the gun safe. "About?"

"The bullying case."

He smiled and headed to the kitchen. "You don't have to give me sources or anything, Sam. I talked with Nikki and her parents this evening."

"Good, but that's not what I want to tell you."

Dad leaned and kissed Mom's neck. "I don't know which smells better, the plate you made for me or your perfume."

Oh, gross. "Dad!"

Mom laughed. "You'd better give her your attention, or she's going to burst." She handed Dad a large glass of iced tea.

"Okay, then. At least let me sit down." He pulled out the kitchen chair opposite where Sam stood and sat at the table. "I'm all ears."

"Jefferson Cole." The muscles in her body kept tensing of their own accord. Probably trying to keep up with her racing mind.

"Nikki's brother?"

She nodded.

"What about him?" Dad took a sip of tea.

"It's him." She grinned wide and shifted her weight from one foot to the other.

Dad set down his glass. "Jefferson's the bully?"

Sam nodded. "It all makes sense."

"Okay, I'll play devil's advocate for you. What's his motive?"

"To get his and Nikki's parents back together."

Dad crossed his arms over his chest. "Sit down and explain."

"I can't sit." She gripped the back of the chair across the table from him. "When I interviewed Jefferson, he told me that even though his dad had moved out, as soon as Jefferson hurt his ankle, his dad was back all the time. Even Nikki said that her parents stopped fighting when they came together over their kids."

Sam straightened and paced toward the window. "He saw that if he could put him or Nikki in crisis, their parents would come together in a peaceful way, which made him think maybe they would stop divorce proceedings. Nikki said they hadn't talked about seeing the lawyer in weeks."

Dad nodded slowly. "Okay, give me your rundown of how all the clues tie to Jefferson being the bully."

"Okay." She let out a long breath. "How did he get the diet bars in her locker? She told me more than once that only she and Aubrey know the combination, but when I was at her house, she told me she couldn't remember passwords or anything, so she wrote everything down in her paper notebook. That's how he knew her combination, and how he knew her login and password to the EAST computers."

Again, Dad nodded.

Sam continued. "He knew he couldn't send the email from their family computer, so he had to find another. One that wouldn't trace back to him or one of his friends. He probably got the idea to use the EAST lab computers because of the article Nikki did several weeks ago about how it was fashionable to know all the cool programs available in EAST."

She pulled out the chair across the table from her father and sat. "He knew the back way into the school by the baseball diamond because he spent a lot of time this summer at the pool at Chalamont Park with a friend." She smiled. "He also owns a green Schwinn bicycle."

"Nice." Dad grinned as Mom set the plate she'd saved for him on the table in front of him. "What about the diet pills?"

Sam laughed. "That's easy, Dad. He used the family computer to order the pills. Since their mom is probably like you, she keeps her billing info stored, so when he ordered it, he just clicked to confirm it, and the order was concluded."

"You've done well, Sam. I'm impressed. Seems you've got all the loose ends covered."

"No, there's still one out there. The text sent to her phone. I haven't figured that one out yet."

Dad grinned. "I can help you with that. It was a go-phone, untraceable, and belongs to his best friend."

"Ahh. At least I didn't miss — " Sam stared at her father. "You already knew all this?"

He nodded. "Jefferson confessed when Buster and I went to talk to Mr. and Mrs. Cole this evening."

"Why didn't you tell me?"

Dad chuckled. "You didn't exactly give me a chance, Sam." He took a bite of his dinner, then swallowed. "But you nailed everything perfectly. You should be very proud of yourself. That was some great detective work." He took a sip of tea and grinned. "Are you sure you don't want to be a cop instead of a measly, nosy reporter?"

"Hey!" Mom threw the kitchen towel across the room and hit Dad in the head.

He laughed and tossed it back to her. "Just kidding."

Mom came and joined them at the table. "I think you both solved the case beautifully."

"Dad, what's going to happen to Jefferson now?"

"Well, we're not going to charge him with bullying, since it was his sister, and he's got more issues to face, but he will have to face the consequences of stealing the computers from school."

Stealing was wrong, Sam knew that, but she couldn't help feeling sorry for Jefferson. He'd gone to some serious lengths to get his parents to stay a couple. Being punished hardly seemed fair to a kid who was just fighting to keep his family together.

"Hey, I know what you're thinking, but he broke the

law. He stole property that belonged to the school. Remember how upset you were when you heard they'd been stolen? You take EAST so you know how important they are."

"I know." And she did. She just hated that Jefferson had been so desperate to keep his parents together that he'd hurt his sister, broken into the school, and stolen computers.

"Buster and I said in our reports that since the computers were recovered, we would recommend counseling and probation."

Sam smiled. Man, her dad rocked! "So that's what he'll get?"

Dad shrugged. "It's not up to us, but the juvenile court usually puts a lot of weight on our reports."

"I hope so."

"Now, what the school does is a totally different matter."

"What do you mean?" Sam asked.

"He broke a slew of rules by breaking in and stealing the computers that all have grounds for expulsion."

Oh, no! "Surely Mrs. Trees isn't going to expel him."

"I don't know. I know he'll definitely be suspended, at the least. She has to punish him, Sam."

"It's just so … sad."

"It is," Mom said, "but even though he thought he had a good reason for what he did, he still broke school rules and the law. He's confessed, which is a good start, but has to pay the price for what he did."

Speaking of confessing to breaking school rules ... Sam took a deep breath. "Mom and Dad, I have something I need to tell you."

"What? You can tell us anything."

Yeah, he said that *now*. "Well, I kinda broke a big school rule, too." She went on to explain how she'd looked at the EAST roster on Mrs. Trees' computer. "I didn't steal anything and didn't hack into a file or anything, but I know what I did was wrong."

"It was." Dad swallowed, then finished off his tea. "I think tomorrow morning, you should report to Mrs. Trees' office and tell her."

"What if she kicks me off the paper? Or the cheer squad?" Sam's stomach looped into knots. "What if she suspends or expels me?"

"We'll deal with whatever your punishment is, my sweet girl."

Dad pushed back his chair. "You can start by doing the dishes, then heading on to bed." He stood. "I can't say I'm not a little disappointed in what you did, Sam, but I'm proud of you for telling us when you didn't have to. Goodnight."

Sam finished loading the dishwasher, then turned it on. She took Chewy out for a final walk before bed. The stars shone brightly in the clear sky. Sam sat on the back porch steps and stared up at them.

God, I know we're supposed to pray for Your will, but if You could, it'd be really awesome if you didn't let Jefferson get too much punishment. I might've done the same thing for my parents. It'd be nice if you helped Mr. and Mrs. Cole repair their marriage so their family could stay together.

Chewy chased a June bug buzzing around the light by the kitchen door.

Speaking of families staying together ... I'm okay if Mom decides to take the National Geographic *gig. I'm choosing to believe you'll keep her safe, and you'll watch out for me and Dad while she's gone.*

Chewy ran up to Sam, rubbed against her leg and whined. Sam laughed and stood, giving the dog a quick rub between the ears.

Kinda like Chewy here is afraid of the dark, but okay if I'm out here with her — I'm scared of Mom going, but I'm okay because I know you're here with me.

● ● ●

"A whole week of cleaning up Mrs. Trees' office? That isn't too rough," Makayla told Sam.

Sam shook her head. "Not at all. It won't be part of my record, and I'm not penalized in cheer or anything. She said it took a lot of guts to come tell her what I did, and she appreciated that." Sam grinned. "Of course, I told her it was my dad's idea, but she said I didn't have to tell her that, which still shows good character."

Makayla laughed. "I'm just glad you're not in serious trouble."

"Me, too. I have enough trouble about to hit me." Sam shut her locker and waited on Makayla.

"You haven't seen Aubrey at all today?"

"Nope. Not looking forward to seeing her now."

"Well, you don't want to be tardy and get sent to the office. Mrs. Trees might not be so generous with your consequences next time." Makayla shut her locker and gave Sam a quick hug. "Good luck. Now get going."

Sam drug her feet as she headed into last period. She'd managed to stay in a pretty good mood all day, but now … just knowing she would see Aubrey made her almost sick to her stomach. She let out a sigh and headed into class just as the tardy bell rang.

"Well, how nice of you to join us," Aubrey said as soon as she cleared the threshold.

It was going to be a very long class today.

Nikki came up and gave Sam a big hug. "Your dad is pretty awesome. He went out of his way to not only write a recommendation that Jefferson not get thrown in juvie, but he gave my parents the name of a good, Christian marriage counselor."

Dad had left out that little nugget of information. Yeah, her dad was pretty cool. "I'm glad. I hope it all works out."

"Me, too." Nikki turned to stare at Aubrey, then back at Sam. "Look, I know you two don't really like each other — "

That was putting it mildly.

" — but you both are really good people. The whole newspaper staff has gotten together, and we'd like to ask you both to put the past behind us and move forward. Together. Without you two being at odds."

Sam noticed everyone staring at them, waiting. She licked her lips. "Aubrey, I'm sorry for being so rude to you. Nikki was upset, and I should have concentrated on her, not you."

The room held a collective breath as Aubrey stood still. And silent.

Kevin Haynes joined them, standing beside Sam. "We really don't want there to be any more awkwardness. Thanks, Sam, for apologizing."

Aubrey blushed. "Oh, I'm sorry, too. Let's just move on."

Everyone burst into applause. Sam had to refrain from asking if everyone believed that apology was sincere.

Nikki grinned and followed Aubrey to the editor's desk.

"Well played, do-gooder."

Sam turned around to face Felicia Adams. She smiled. "What are you doing here, troublemaker?"

Felicia returned the grin. "It seems my mother had

a change of heart and agreed to let me at least participate in the school paper." She shrugged. "It's a start."

"How'd you get Mrs. Trees to agree to it?"

Felicia laughed. "After a very long meeting with her
and my mom, I promised to have a 4.0 by the end of the
first semester and to not get another referral. If I do, I'm
outta here."

"Nice. Well, welcome to the Senator Speak. I guess
you met Aubrey, our editor."

"Oh, yeah. Real piece of work there."

Sam chuckled. "Hey, I'm trying to be nice here."

"Good luck with that." Felicia laughed.

Sam realized she really enjoyed being around Felicia.
It was nice to have her as a friend.

"Attention students," Mrs. Trees' voice came over
the intercom. "We're pleased to announce your Robinson Middle School Homecoming Queen is ..."

Sam sensed a hush fall over the entire school.

"Remy Tucker. Congratulations, Queen Remy."

The noise level rose. Lana shrugged as Celeste told
her she was sorry she didn't make it.

Sam noticed Aubrey gave Nikki a hug, and she
couldn't help but wonder if that was for Nikki's sake or
Aubrey's.

Sam raised her eyebrows and tilted her head.

"Stop thinking them thoughts, do-gooder, or you
might end up eating that apology."

CHAPTER TWENTY

"Sam, my sweet girl, can you please come in here and sit down?" Mom hollered from the living room.

This was it. Mom had finally made her decision.

"Coming." Sam let out a slow breath. *I'm trusting you, Lord. I'll be okay with whatever she's decided, just like I said.* And she meant that.

Change couldn't be stopped, but Sam was pretty sure God didn't want humans to just stay the same. He wanted everyone to grow and learn and grow some more. You couldn't grow if you weren't willing to change.

She sat on the big, comfy chair catty-corner to the couch where Mom and Dad sat together. A unified front. "Look, Mom, before you say anything, can I say something first?"

"Sure."

"I don't know what you've decided, but I want you to know, whether you go or not, it's up to you. Whatever your decision, I'm okay with it. Really."

Mom glanced at Dad, then smiled at her. "You're sure? No matter if I'm gone for the full six months, you're okay with that?"

"I'll miss you, but yeah. I'm fine with it." Sam checked her feelings and realized she really and truly was okay.

"Well, you won't have to figure it out because I turned it down."

"What? I thought it was a once-in-a-lifetime opportunity that wouldn't come around again." She could only hope Mom didn't turn it down because of how she thought Sam would react if she accepted.

"I thought so, but I had my own reservations about going. I talked with Pastor Patterson. I prayed. Your dad and I prayed together. And finally, I realized it wasn't as important to me as my family. You and your dad are the most important people in the whole world to me, and I'd rather be with you two than anywhere else in the world. The idea of it was nice, and I'm honored they offered it to me, but it was truly my choice to turn them down."

Sam flew around the coffee table and hugged Mom, then pulled Dad in. She truly had some awesome parents.

… The entire Senator Speak editorial staff is proud of our own Samantha Sanderson for keeping her word and protecting her reporting sources despite the possibility of dire

personal consequences. Congratulations, Sam, on a job well done. Sound off, Senators. Leave a comment with your thoughts. ~ Aubrey Damas, *Editor in Chief*, reporting

ACKNOWLEDGMENTS

My most heartfelt thanks to my editor, Kim Childress, who holds my hand and cheers me on! Working with you is a pure joy, and I feel blessed to have you in my corner as we share Sam and her friends with the world.

There are so many people involved with the making of a book. I am so thankful to the whole team at Zonderkidz for helping the Samantha Sanderson series come to life. Every person has been such a delight to work with.

Special thanks to Robinson Middle School who let me share how special they are with the rest of the world. I played around with possibilities and lay of the land as I saw fit. Any mistakes in the representation of details are mine, where I twisted in the best interest of my story.

HUGE thanks to my awesome agent, Steve Laube (HP), for everything you do for me, from giving me career advice to talking me off the proverbial ledge. You are awesome!

My extended family members are my biggest fans and greatest cheerleaders. Thank you for ALWAYS being in my corner: Mom, BB and Robert, Bek and Krys,

Bubba and Lisa, Brandon, Rachel, and Aunt Millicent. Especially my Papa, whom I love and miss every day.

I couldn't do what I do without my girls — Emily Carol, Remington Case, and Isabella Co-Ceaux. I love each of you so much! Your support and encouragement mean everything to me. And to my precious grandsons, Benton and Zayden. You are joys in my life.

I can't imagine doing what I do without my true partner in life, Case. You make me smile when I'm ready to scream and laugh when I really want to cry. Thank you for always believing in me, even when I don't believe in myself. I love you. Always.

Finally, all glory to my Lord and Savior, Jesus Christ. I can do all things through Him who gives me strength.

DISCUSSION QUESTIONS

1. Bullying is a very serious issue. Discuss how bullying makes people feel. Do you know what your school's policy is against bullying? Find out.

2. Jefferson went to serious lengths in hopes to keep his parents together. Do you think he should have been punished for bullying his sister? Why or why not?

3. Sam's parents prayed together when an important family decision needed to be made. What does the Bible tell us about praying together? (See Matthew 18:20 for discussion.)

4. Nikki and Jefferson were upset about their parents getting divorced. How do you feel about the issue?

5. Homecoming is a fun time for most schools. How does your school enjoy homecoming?

6. Aubrey was clearly jealous of Nikki, her own best friend, for being nominated to homecoming court. Have you ever felt jealous of one of your friends? How did you deal with the situation? Discuss ways you can work through your emotions rather than avoiding your friend like Aubrey did.

7. When Sam's mother considers taking a long-term job out of town, Sam has a lot of inner turmoil over it. Has one of your family members ever had to be away from family for a long period of time? What are ways families who are separated for a time can still feel connected?

8. Jefferson did some really mean things to his sister to make her feel bad about herself. What does the Bible tell you about how you're made? (See Genesis 5:1 for discussion.)

9. Felicia was branded a troublemaker, but she seems to be coming around. Do you think people can change? Why or why not?

10. Sam and Makayla are bestest buddies. Who is your bestest friend? What do you enjoy doing together?

11. Many families have to move and find new schools or church families. Have you ever had to move? How did you feel? Discuss ways you can make newcomers feel welcome in your school and church.

12. If you were a student at RMS, who would you most want to be friends with? Why?